MW01226547

LIBERTY
SHIP TRIP

Steaming West To The Far East

HOWARD VENEZIA

CONTENTS

FORWARD

If this novel strikes you as if it is dwelling on the experiences and feelings of an immature fellow engaged in the *sea going profession,* it is coming across the way I intended it to. It is not his first time on a ship, nor is it his first time in being awash in interludes with the "seedier", waterfront ensconced individuals that prey on mostly inexperienced youngsters earning their living on commercial ships.

You will note that while having been in the "going to sea" trade for two years, our hero is still ill-equipped to handle some of the job or locale related inter- personal drama that comes his way. You may not agree with his actions arising from this interplay, but those actions reflect his being in the "learning process". Further, this book carries him away from a deep familiarity with the early 1950's tank-ship trade, as a Qualified Member of the Engineering Department moving petroleum products, to a new experience with a "dry cargo" carrying, WW II vintage vessel; a reciprocating steam-engine driven Liberty Ship. Our hero here is on a steep learning curve regarding his primary reason for being aboard; to properly keep the ship "steaming". Effort was taken in this regard, to ensure readers' technical familiarity with his work on board the ship and with his "novice view" of the places he visits as part of the ship crew.

Our hero is also on a learning curve for interactions with ladies he meets in the overseas ports his ship calls upon. Like it or not, "fleshpots" visited by seamen when "on liberty", exist. And like most young seamen on strictly budgeted liberty time, our hero seeks them out. His experiences here vary.

Please enjoy the story, and while as much of it is related to facts generally observed in the "seagoing world", it is only lightly tied to actual events experienced or witnessed by the author. Its tie to actual persons is not intended and would be purely coincidental.

/s/ Howard Venezia

CHAPTER ONE

A DAY IN BEAUMONT

It was a sunny, hot and sticky East Texas, late summer mid-day and Merchant Seaman, Joey Vicenzo, was fist fighting with a Beaumont, Texas, "Wobbly" (International Workers of the World Union) member stevedore, named Les. They were taking vicious swings at each other's head. Of note, they were just a half block down College Street from their most recent "overnight stay" in the Drunk Tank at the Police Station in Beaumont.

This fight actually started the night before at a whorehouse on neighboring Post Office Street, and … because of the fight's location and its potentially adverse affect on the "house's" business, the house Madam called the cops. This complaint by the Madam resulted in the two fight participants winding up in the new Jail Drunk Tank.

From the night before, Joey had a reddish and swollen lump above and to the right of his right eye…but he was unmarked, so far, this day. He actually was doing quite well in the altercation and had given the longshoreman a cut and swollen lip. Both had worked up a sweat by the time a police squad car, on its way to the Station House, pulled up alongside them. The fatter and physically larger of the two squad car cops tried (unsuccessfully) to get between the fighters and "restore the public order". He knew the two participants from his "check-in briefing" at the Station House that morning and was calling to them by name in his efforts to stop the fight. What came out in fluid "Texican" was;

"Damn it, Joaay. Y'all want to get booked ag'in…an' wind up wif more dan a ord'nance violashun on yer sheet? Now… Break it up, dammit!" At about that time the cop's partner had succeeded in getting positioned directly in front of Les and with that action, stopped the fight.

Fight over and with the police at the scene, Joey immediately turned and continued down College Street toward the waterfront…while Les remained at the fight scene trying to explain that the fight was; "…really not my fault. That sumbitch is gett'n between me an' mah gal, Betty, over at *the house* on Post Office Street…" and so forth. Hearing all this, Joey reflected on his status with Betty, and confirmed that he and Les were "in the same boat" with her. Both men thought they were in a "serious relationship" with the whore, Betty.

Now, Betty was a very attractive and slender brunette with a sexually suggestive gait and rather large breasts. She preferred tight Gypsy-style blouses with colorful and equally tight skirts. She wore her naturally curly hair short and conforming in profile to her head. The seams on her nylons were perfectly positioned, running up the center of her well-formed calves and her "business dress" had her wearing medium height high heeled shoes. Combining all these "attractive" attributes with her age being in the lower to mid-twenties, she was close to being the most sought after "red light" attraction in Beaumont. Joey had become a good customer when ships he was sailing on were in Beaumont and because of that, Betty began showing a bit of partiality toward him.

As a point of interest, during one of the couple's conversational interludes, Betty had confided in depth to Joey. She had explained away her *heavily covered with make-up* facial scar that ran diagonally from right temple, then across the bridge of her nose to her left cheekbone, as being the result of an auto accident she was in while "running away from the police" *in a stolen car*…when she was a teenager. That law breaking episode did not end until she was released from the female prison at Huntsville, Texas, a few years later. Following Huntsville, Betty seemed to continue her association with the seedier part of the Gulf Coast, East Texas society. A recent "boyfriend" introduced her to a pimp who didn't treat her too well. Another of that pimp's girls told her about the relative benefits of being under a madam rather than a pimp and specifically mentioned the Beaumont whorehouse and now here she was, at the "house" in Beaumont.

No matter what her background and character was, Joey had fallen for her and over time, and had talked himself into thinking the feeling was mutual on her part. In that assumption he was only partially correct. Betty was, after all, *in the "whore house business" to make money and all else was secondary to that.*

Still walking downhill, Joey did some rethinking about where he was physically heading and now thought he really should see Betty and solidify his relationship with her if possible. He rationalized; "After all, I wanted to be spending today and next week with her "on a vacation" of sorts…for both of us." He immediately altered course to the Post Office Street "house".

With Post Office Street running right down to the Beaumont waterfront, Joey couldn't help but see a "riding high"(holding no cargo) Liberty Ship readying to be tied up at the deep water docking wharf, on the waterfront extending seaward from the "bottom of the street". Being a "career (so far) oil-carrying-tanker-bound seaman", his professional interest in the dry cargo carrying Liberty was fleeting.

Upon arriving at the "house", Joey went through the entrance and into the couch-filled foyer where two of "the girls" were having lunch; sandwiches and Coca Colas. The heavier of the two, a blond girl in a house robe called Alicia, knew Joey and in Texanese, welcomed him into the house. "Here a bit early, ain't ya? Here fo' lunch…or what, Joey?" Joey appreciated being welcomed into the house and came back with; "Am some hungry but really came to see Betty. Food'll come soon enough. Think she's available this early in the day?" Alicia nodded that Betty was up and around and volunteered to; "…fetch her".

Betty appeared within a minute or two and was dressed comfortably in loose fitting Jeans, "go-ahead" slippers and a "bare midriff" blouse with the shirt-tails tied off in a knot in front. Ever attractive in Joey's eyes, Betty actually looked like a youngish Texas housewife… spending a quiet day. Joey didn't want an audience listening in to what he had to say to Betty, so asked if they could go to somewhere more private to speak. Betty suggested her room but told Joey straight up that that

3

would cost him the "short time" rate…adding; "Gotta keep the Madam happy, you know." Joey unhappily shrugged; "OK!"

Once in the room, Joey told her of him and Les spending the previous night in the Drunk Tank as the result of the madam's call and then, upon release, the two of them picking up where they had left off; fighting again. Betty took the news seriously. Her demeanor somewhat subdued, she apologized to Joey for "her part" in the altercation. In the following conversation where Joey was hoping he'd get her to show her favoritism for him, she did not even hint that she would give up Les in favor of keeping Joey close. Joey was somewhat dismayed by her lack of taking a *favorable* position regarding this "most serious" situation. Further, knowing that this conversation was costing him the "short time" rate, Joey had been considering taking Betty to bed there and then…but was "turned off" by her over all business "callousness". He suddenly wanted not only for the conversation to end, but also to be out of her sight and out of the room. He mumbled that he'd call again, but for the time being, he'd just leave "the house"… and have something to eat. He left Betty sitting on the bed.

CHAPTER TWO

THE SHAPE UP

Back on Post Office Street Joey continued ambling toward the waterfront and where he was staying, Captain D's Lodging & Bar-and-Grill establishment. Now hungry, he went into the bar and found a stool at the bar from which to order a ham and cheese sandwich with a glass of beer. Since Captain D's was the town's main "watering hole" for seamen and dockworkers, Joey had little trouble getting into a conversation with another tanker seaman,... this one an Able Bodied Seaman (AB) who also worked for SOCONY VACUUM. The conversation with the AB lasted only about an hour since the AB's ship was departing that evening for Paulsboro, New Jersey and he "had to go". In departing, he congratulated Joey on his status as a "...seaman on leave", even if the "leave" had to be in this "shithole town, Beaumont!" While tired from his loss of sleep the night before, Joey opted not to go up to his room, but instead to stay in the bar sipping on another beer.

Joey remained on his stool for the next half hour and was ready to call it an evening and retire when three middle aged men in suits stepped into the now crowded bar. The thin, taller and smiling man in the middle was obviously "the important guy" of the trio. His suit was gray and consisted of a well pressed and well fitting, single-button jacket and slightly pegged trousers. Facially, he sort of resembled a clean shaven Abe Lincoln. He was flanked by two sturdily built, frowning, shorter men who wore rather ill-fitting blue suits with slightly bulging, right-side jacket pockets. The bulges were caused by having these pockets stuffed with "argument-ending" blackjacks, or saps.

Upon their entry, Joey had mentally categorized the three visitors. He correctly thought the two short ones were "Union Goons", or people who fought with and suppressed "strike breakers", if it came to that. He knew strike breakers were those Company-hired men who would cross striker-picket lines to go to work and effectively "break" the strike in the company's favor. The three "suits" got everyone's attention upon their entrance since; "...*no one* wore suits on the Beaumont waterfront..." The taller man strode over to where Joey was sitting and took from a pant pocket a large "pocket ID card" and put the card into his jacket pocket with the lettering on it readable by people in front of him. The card read, in large letters: MFOWW REPRESENTATIVE. Joey's interest in him heightened since the MFOWW was his Union. The taller man then asked Joey if he could use Joey's stool from which to speak to the bar customers. Joey promptly slid off his stool and gestured its availability to the man.

The tall man climbed the stool, leaned a leg against the bar to steady himself, then drew himself up to his full height... and held forth.

"Hello; my name is Charlie Paddock and I'm here to talk to the merchant seamen amongst y'all. Why? Look behind you! Just by looking out the door you can see any ship that ties up to the dry-cargo docks out front. I know some of y'all saw a Liberty ship just a few minutes ago making herself fast to the cargo dock. That ship is the SS CHARLES MC GOWAN. For those of you that have been playing ostrich the past year, we've had a war going on in Korea trying to stop the Red Bastards from the north from taking over the South. *To get the stuff to win that war from here in the States to there, the country has been reactivating those "WW II work horses", the Liberty ships... to carry the needed war cargo.*

Now, I've been involved in two prior local Liberty ship reactivations and my Union, the MFOWW, is sucking hind tit in adequately manning these ships from our central hiring hall. Further, we also just can't seem to get the Oiler and Firemen volunteers from the local, Beaumont Hall, to fill up the watch standing "people needs" for these ships. The "deckies" and the "stew burners" are filling all their slots with ease. I don't know exactly why, but maybe our engineering endorsement- carrying guys get a bit panicked about oiling a reciprocating engine, firing Scotch Boilers and "nurse-maiding" a bunch of auxiliary machinery using Low-Pressure-Steam with reciprocating-drivers. I want all those "nervous" Black Gang troops in here to stop being concerned. We've been collecting past "*WW II engineering recip'- qualified*" people from all over the states to man these ships whenever we can. These "older" folks are now actually the teachers of the newly recruited "turbine-experienced", but "recip'- ignorant" engineers. Y'all should know that our nation and the shipping companies needing the cargo space are depending on getting their Liberties into the war…and **pronto** too! For example, the Liberty ship, the MC GOWAN, tying up in Beaumont today is being managed by American President Lines (APL) and that shipping line has long-standing contracts for manning its ships with the Sailors Union of the Pacific for deck hands, the Marine Cooks and Stewards for the "stew burners" and the MFOWW for their Black Gangs. You West Coast seamen who are experienced with APL know they are "really good" on overtime work and pay …and are great "feeders". Whoever goes aboard the Liberty here can expect that "same care and feeding".

Now, what my Union really needs are Oilers and Firemen ready to sign up on the ship at the docks behind you, outside this bar's door, to go to Korea with a load of military cargo and make some good bucks while they're doing "their thing" for the US of A. Who'll be the first to volunteer?"

Joey, who had been paying close attention to Charlie Paddock throughout the recruiting harangue, was still standing next to the stool Charlie stood on. Further, being somewhat "on the outs" with Bettie, *the Korean interlude …with Oriental women instead of stateside whores to consort with* sounded quite interesting to him. With no further thought he reached over and tugged on Charlie's pant leg. When Charlie looked down on him, Joey said: Hey Shipmate, I'm a "(Union) card carrying" Oiler and I'd like to sign up on that Liberty for the Korean run… problem is; I'm not "reciprocating engine" experienced. Think APL will go along with me signing on to "oil" that thing?

7

Charlie said; "No problem! I guarantee it! Just wait here a couple of minutes to see if I get any other volunteers to go with us, then I'll take you on down to sign Articles for the trip." Joey said; "OK. I'm living here. Let me square up with Captain D on the rent, and pick up my gear... Then I'll be ready to move aboard and get to work." Charlie asked; "How much do you owe? I'll take care of the rent, if'n it ain't too much." The proprietor, Captain D, who had been listening to all that transpired said; "Five bucks will handle the rent...and there are no other charges." Charlie reached into his pant pocket, pulled out a small roll of bills, peeled a fiver off the top, and handed it to Captain D. No other "volunteers" stepped forward in the bar.

Joey departed the bar and headed upstairs to his room to collect his gear. His next stop would be the Liberty and a sea going job for the next several months. He had no second thoughts on what he had just committed to. In his room while collecting his gear he thought again of Betty and his need to let her know what he just did. For one reason or another he knew his shipping out right now might constitute "the final pitfall" for their relationship.

With sea bag and hand-carrying bag both full of his belongings, Joey dropped back downstairs at Captain D's and smiled at the waiting Charlie Paddock. Charlie asked: "Ready?" Joey responded with a nod and then, leaving the two goons in the bar, they both headed down to the waterfront and the waiting Liberty ship. It was cool and for some reason, his full sea bag didn't feel as heavy as it did most times.

Upon arrival at the ship they climbed the accommodation ladder to the main deck where there was an "AB" watch stander ensconced behind a large desk. Before him was the ship's Watch Log and Joey arrived before this desk in time to see Charlie Paddock, with index finger pointing to a space for the next log entry, directing somewhat loudly, that the AB "log in" Joey as reporting aboard for the upcoming trip to Korea and... ready to sign the Foreign (Voyage) Articles, to make it all legal.

The Deck Watch first explained that the Chief Mate took "the articles" along with the Ship's Official Log to bring them up-to-date after the ship's move to the waterfront from the upriver anchorage. The

Mate returned at that time with the Log in hand and presented it to the AB. The AB did as Charlie directed and logged Joey on board; "… for the voyage to Korea and then back to the United States…" All this was logged after having Joey's last name, Vicenzo, spelled to him twice!

CHAPTER THREE

HIS FIRST LIBERTY SHIP

As now a member the ship's company, Joey still had to be led to the engineering berthing area and to his designated watch berthing space in that area. Charlie did the required guiding. While the Engineering Berthing was similar to that found on the tankers and was situated on the starboard side, main deck and within the ship's "house", the actual layout of the crew's berthing spaces differed from those Joey was used to in the tankers. Here his "room" had a name plate over the joiner doorway designating the space for the "12 – 4 Watch" and the room itself appeared larger than those for unlicensed-personnel berthing on T-2 tankers.

The room had a set of bunk-beds, two lockers, a double sink and enough cabinet and locker space for him and his watch mate, the Watch Fireman/Water-tender, to empty their luggage bags into. Joey was not surprised to see that the lower bunk was already "taken" as its bedding was thoroughly messed up. "So be it ..." he thought. "Them's that're here first, gets first pickings." He tossed his sea and tote bags into the room corner that was closest to the standing lockers. The Union Representative, his "guiding" of Joey over with and with the salutation to Joey of, "Hope you have the best of luck on this trip"; then departed the ship.

Since his berthing space was just across the ship's starboard passageway from the Engine Mess, Joey made his way into the Mess

10

for a sandwich and cold drink. Enroute to the Mess from his berthing space, he noticed a name plate over another set of joiner doors that identified the doorway as the access, from the main deck, to the ship's Engine Room. As he expected, and as it was on tankers, the sandwich and drink makings were on one of the tables in the Mess. While eating his sandwich he thought he heard some *hammer on steel* noises coming up from the engineering spaces, and he decided to investigate their source.

His view of the Engine Room (ER) from the upper ladder level was close to completely including the engine's Main Operating Station, which was on the starboard side of the engine. Immediately forward of this big reciprocating steam engine were the two boiler fronts. All this machinery was on the ER's lowest level. What he also saw in his "engine space viewing" was a tall, thin fellow with ball-peen hammer in hand, in jeans, wearing a loose shirt and a blue ball cap, and talking to a heavy set, big man wearing clean khaki work clothes. Both men had their full attention on the starboard boiler's water level glass gauge. The boilers had been lit-off and the forced-draft blowers located amidships at Joey's level were running, and making their normal, high-pitched, loud blower-whine. He had become "comfortably" accustomed to "blower whine" on steaming tankers. Their noise was comforting, since when they stopped whining, the engine was normally shut-down and… there was usually something seriously wrong in the engine room.

At about that time, an older, thin and smaller fellow wearing what can be best described as a railroad engineer's striped grey, cover-all outfit, rounded the engine front from the port side and began gesturing to the other two. The "other two" who Joey believed to be the Watch Engineer and Fireman, both disappeared to do what the "railroad-guy" wanted to have done. Joey determined the "hierarchy of the folks below" that he was watching, to be: the one in the railroad outfit was probably the Chief Engineer, the one in clean khakis was probably the Engineer on Watch and the one in jeans and loose-fitting clothes either the Fireman or Oiler on Watch. He was almost "right on" with his observations. Further, he observed correctly that the Chief was supervising the concurrent light-off of the engineering plant supporting or Auxiliary Machinery. Joey immediately rationalized that since the ship had just been delivered "dead stick", dock-side by tugs that took her from the upriver, ship-storage anchorage, her "boiler and Auxiliary Machinery light-off" was needed to now allow the ship to become self-sufficient in all respects. Joey thought the entire situation was "healthy" for the ship. He also thought; 'Probably all that remained to be done prior to the ship departing for points South and West to Panama, then to Korea, was for the Skipper to arrange having the ship's consumables… and cargo delivered and stored. These "consumables" would include; her fuel oil, potable water, and (consumable) food stores; all to be delivered and stowed on board. Joey surmised that all these needs plus the start of her loading cargo would be satisfied within the next few days.

Joey was toying with the thought that while he was the 12 – 4 Oiler and didn't have to be on Watch until midnight, *he "really didn't know his butt about oiling reciprocating main engines and… mostly reciprocating engine-driven* auxiliary machinery and so, he needed to be educated on that stuff…and quickly too! He turned to depart the engine room upper flats to go to his berthing space and shift into his work clothes and then drop back into the engine room…to learn.

At that time, swinging around onto the upper platform from the starboard passageway…and directly in front of him, completely blocking his way, was o*ne of the largest men he had ever seen! Saying that the fellow was built like a "fully mature redwood tree trunk" was too conservative in describing his size. He was huge!* His jet black hair was cropped short, in almost a "military cut", and it crowned a normal sized head… but that was where his "normalcy" ended. His height was in the neighborhood of 6 feet, three or four inches, and his weight, while housing little fat, was well over three hundred pounds. Joey had to look twice to see the man's neck as it seemed to disappear into his shoulders, but there it was, surrounded by his red and black checkered work shirt collar, and located under his head. His neck looked to Joey to be as big around as a woman's waist! The work shirt was buttoned, however because of his chest size, the buttoning started at about the fourth button down with the upper part fanning out toward the shoulders and displaying a relatively clean under shirt beneath it. The shirt was tucked into a pair of jeans so large at the waist that Joey, falling back on a Brooklynese derogatory phrase, jokingly thought the jeans had to be made by "Omar the Tent Maker". Keeping these pants in place was a belt of 21-thread hemp rope running through the belt loops and tied off in a square knot in front. Joey didn't bother to look down to ascertain what *the giant* was using for footwear, since his mind was focusing on how and where the big fellow was able to buy *any clothes* that fit him.

The big man saw Joey staring at him somewhat dumbfoundedly and started to smile. He said; "My name is Tom Rodgers but most folks call me Big Tom…or just Tom for short. And while I'm good sized, I'm not the biggest in my family. I've got one younger brother who plays football "on the line", for the New York Giants and who, while younger than me, is both taller and outweighs me. Had another brother who didn't take a back seat to either of us. He was killed during the war. He was a marine and fought in the South Pacific and was killed on Okinawa. *Took a while for me to tolerate Japs since finding that out.*"

Sobering up, Big Tom smilingly said: "Now, I'm the 8 – 12 Oiler and I'll be the dude that wakes you for the Watch and you'll be relieving me. You don't look old enough to be Liberty-ship-experienced, so I suggest you let me take you on a typical Oiler "watch round" before you try to relieve me. Joey thought; 'This answers the mail on getting me up to speed on making Watch Rounds on this Liberty!' His only comment to Big Tom was; "Let's do it and while we're making our way around, I'll bring you up to date on my background. Also, I'm a pretty fast learner, so *unless I ask you a question on what you're pointing out to me, assume I've got it!*

CHAPTER FOUR

BEING EDUCATED IS GOOD

On the way down the ladder from the Upper Flats, Big Tom pointed out to Joey; that between the two Forced Draft Blowers on the upper Engine Room deck was a grease gun and a stash of cylinder oil and graphite grease mixed in a big bucket with a brush protruding from the bucket. "This is the most important tool you'll use in making your Watch rounds. On a Liberty ship, virtually all "Auxiliaries", either topside or down here in the Engine Room, are in reality, being driven by small reciprocating steam engines. As such, they'll all take the cylinder oil and graphite grease to the packing in their con-rod shaft "unit stuffing box". The Main Engine, on the other hand, takes aimed, straight lube oil to its "catch pans". The lube oil is then "tubed and wicked" from the pans to where it's needed at the bearings.

They then made it down to the Upper Engine Flats and while pointing to several lube oil catch pans that would be fed LO from the hand-applicator squirt-cans, Tom asked Joey; "See what I meant by catch pans and feed tubing?" Joey nodded his understanding. Big Tom immediately came back with: "Let's make believe this is your Watch Round so go ahead and do the "oiling". Joey did as told…and got a much better feel for what consisted "hand-lubing" on this ship. They continued this "LO & graphite grease" and just plain "LO" lubing for the remainder of Joey's first Watch Round.

Tom's tutorial also included the "novel" but correct method of lubing the engine connecting-rod (con-rod) "cross-head-follower guides". These procedures came into play when the engine was running and included applying a "soon-to-be-emulsified lubricating oil and water mixture via a "Flit Gun" to the flat follower-guides. Tom then displayed on the stopped engine the "quaint" but also proper method of checking to insure that the bearings from wrist-pin to crankshaft were getting properly lubed. This "check" required, while the engine was running, intruding one's fingers into the space between the crank shaft and both the upper and lower wrist-pin bearing shells to obtain "oil samples" This was done to "feel for" any bearing overheating. If there is overheating, the oiler would "feel" a "coffee ground texture" in a "very warm" oil sample he took from the bearing.

Tom emphasized that that on a running engine this procedure required; "… perfect timing between the hand movements and the turning (at a normal 76 RPM) crankshaft". Joey stuck his extended fingers into the designated bearing spaces, saw that they fit…and then, just nodded.

Following this in-depth, virtually "all inclusive" lesson by Tom, Joey then felt somewhat "qualified" to perform as a "Reciprocating Engine Oiler". Watching Joey's face closely to visually see his *understanding of what he was being told*, Tom then said; "We're OK down here, below. Now let's go up topside and practice "Oiling" the Deck Machinery and the Steering Engine." The next half hour was spent with Joey doing just that; the full lubrication of all the ship's Auxiliary and Deck Machinery.

Following his first round and taking departure from Big Tom, Joey made his way back down to the ME (Main Engine) Operating Level and reported to the Second Assistant Engineer (the 12- 4 Watch Engineer) on his completing his First Round under Big Tom's tutelage. The Second Assistant asked if he now "felt comfortable" with the "watch oiler" requirements. Joey replied that Tom was a fine teacher and that he, Joey, was very "comfortable" with what was expected of him. At that time Joey noticed that the gent near the boiler fronts, who was in those loose fitting working clothes, waved the "Hi" sign to him. Joey had previously assumed this was "his partner", the Mid-Watch Fireman and Water- Tender, and he was correct in that assumption. Joey took the lead in the introduction between the two of them by walking over to the boiler watch station.

Joey started the conversation with; "I'm Joey Vicenzo and they call me Joey. Think we're 12-4 room and watch mates and I'm happy with that...and I think you ought to know that up to now, I've been "earning my keep" by Firing and Oiling in the engine rooms of mostly turbo-electric plant, T-2 tankers. This is my first Liberty ...and I guess, in comparison, I'm pretty ignorant on how to oil this ship"

The thin Fireman responded in a Texas drawl with; "Ah'm known as Slim even if'n mah name is Johnny Hooper... an' ah'm fum Houston. Happy to be having you as mah Watch Mate...an' any time y'all want more info on these "Recip' Beasts", just ask. Y'all oughta know; ah've got a lot a' World War Two time on these buckets. An' *they're a bit different fum those turbines y'all u've been with.*" Joey came back with; "Thanks for the offer. Think I'll be taking you up on it long before we're finished with this trip."

Back with the Second, the two Operating Station watch standers left the engine room and made the short trip topside to look for the Fuel Oil (FO) Barge. Since the ship was, in most respects, "making preparations for getting underway", almost after the fact, Joey asked the Engineer whether he had "any word" on when they'd start loading and fueling "out" for the trip to Korea. The Second allowed he was only privy to the same rumors everyone was "kicking around" in that area of interest, but with the boiler and the main engine room light-off already behind them, all it really took was for the fuel barge to come along side and for them to; "...top the tanks off and we Engineers would be ready to leave Beaumont." He went on with; "As far as we in the plant are concerned, all the skipper has to do is say; "Let's go!"...and we're gone!" Glancing around again to the harbor inlet, the Second added; "Matter of fact, we should be getting the FO Barge any time now."

Almost on cue, the tug with the FO Barge came around a point of land and into the harbor, and made for the Liberty. To insure the barge's cargo of Bunker-C fuel oil would actually flow into the Liberty's tanks, Joey knew the cargo would have to have been heated. That was what

Joey checked for on the arriving barge and he saw that the "donkey boiler" topside on the barge had been lit-off and its steam output had been piped by the barge personnel to the barge's cargo holds/tanks to heat its fuel-cargo. There was smoke arising from the barge's boiler.

The Second said to Joey; "Now that you're here topside with me, you can help me with the fueling. It'll be easy since I had Big Tom break out the ship's fueling hose and line-up to fill some of the fuel tanks in the double bottoms, all when he was on watch;…so all we've got to do now is hook-up to the barge and start taking the stuff aboard."

Joey had no problem with the fueling evolution and was pleased that the fueling hoses were the newer kind that had in-hose grounding leads and straps installed… and terminating at the brass couplings at both hose ends. This safety feature, while common on tankers, had not been back-fitted on all the WW II Liberties, and not having grounded hoses would've been of concern to "tanker man" Joey. The fuel came aboard without problems and when the FO Storage tanks were filled, the line-up was shifted to top-off the FO Service tanks in the ship's "boiler room". Joey went below to handle that FO Service Tank filling evolution while the Second stayed top side with the tug.

The tug and barge were released when fueling was completed. Joey noted in passing that during the fueling the APL reputation for being a good "feeding company" was widely recognized. It was with smiles when Joey saw the tug boat seamen taking turns dropping into the Engine Mess for sandwiches and drinks. They did this all the while the fueling operation was going on. The tug-boaters were notably in good spirits upon their return to their boat and that pleased also Joey. He thought "smiling" to generally be a good omen, and recalled that almost all the folks he ran into on this Liberty ship were in good moods today… and smiling. He now smiled as well!

At the Beaumont dry-cargo loading dock, Joey got his answer on their stores and rations "load out". The skipper must have radioed ahead for the where-with-all for those final but critically important items to be promptly delivered to the ship; since they were now seamlessly being delivered by truck almost before Joey had thought of the evolution. Joey also noted that outboard of the stores and rations trucks were other trucks competing for longshoremen attention. These were loaded with the main ship's cargo (tons of Texas grown rice) in 50 lb sacks, stacked on pallets. Some inefficiency in the load-out already existed since, if not involved with loading cargo directly into the ship's cargo-loading apparatus and nets, many stevedores in yellow, white and green helmets were just milling about the cargo-carrying trucks. This lolly-gagging not-withstanding since there was still good "daylight remaining", the cargo-loading would continue unabated through dinner time.

Joey thought it very interesting that he and Big Tom had actually oiled the ship's cargo handling winches and other deck machinery to make ready for this cargo loading as part of their watch rounds …without being told to do it. Joey thought; 'Nothing like having "prior Liberty ship-experienced" dudes like Big Tom on board. He probably saved us a good portion of a day in "our making ready to get underway"!'

Following his relief at 4 PM as the Oiler on Watch, Joey went into his berthing space to clean up and "go ashore" since he thought he had to talk to Betty "about their future". "His world" had certainly changed with his signing "Foreign Articles" on the MC GOWAN and in his rationalizing that Betty deserved being advised on the new status of "their relationship". He had totally forgotten or overlooked that her being a prostitute whose customer base was largely the merchant seamen "hitting the beach" in Beaumont, she had probably in the past, been *overly-exposed* to the last minute "plan changing" that seamen were disposed to engage in.

Since it was still early afternoon when he started up Post Office Street, he just assumed Betty would be unattached and happy and ready to see him when he arrived at the whorehouse. As in the early afternoon the day before, Betty was in one of her "housewife-looking" outfits. And indeed, like a happy housewife, she smilingly welcomed him into the House.

CHAPTER FIVE

DEPARTING BEAUMONT

The conversation with Betty on his upcoming trip went pretty much as Joey had expected. Betty first wanted to know; "If we go into some sort of *you and me* relationship...how am I going to live when you leave? All I can see that lets me eat and sleep comfortably while I wait for you to come back from traipsing around the world, is for you to send me a monthly, or so, allotment check that'll take the place of what I make here. By the way, I'd have to rent an apartment somewhere other than here in Beaumont, since I don't think the cops *would understand* my leaving this house, and still staying here in town. They do take a cut from the house profits and would not tolerate the thought of me going "independent"...and basically, they just wouldn't understand me leaving this House. Don't really know how to say this, but the only way I can see me continuing to earn a buck here or to continue to live here while you're gone, is to continue what I'm now doing!"

Joey had been tiredly leaning back on the bed but he "heard" every word Betty had to say and couldn't come up with an argument to any of her thoughts. He knew he wasn't going to undertake Betty's financial support on a full time basis. Ignoring the major (financial) issue, Joey mumbled that he was definitely leaving on the Liberty... and soon! "No matter what" and was ready to accept a hiatus in their relationship for the period of the upcoming trip. Betty just shrugged. They both then stripped their clothes off and settled into Betty's bed for what they thought was going to be their last shot at love-making. Betty made this tryst "a free one".

After they finished, Joey prepared to leave and provided Betty with his APL Company mailing address. He then got from her the House's mailing address. They promised to exchange letters whenever possible. Joey then left for the ship.

Back on the ship, Joey showered then made for his bunk and a little shut-eye prior to his being called for the Mid Watch. He slept well.

Big Tom made his wake-up call on Joey and Slim at 11:30 PM and told Joey the weather dockside was "clear and cool", or…the message told Joey that he didn't have to dress for inclement weather to make his Topside Rounds. For his watch, Joey then just put on his long sleeve Chino shirt and oil-stained, but clean, jeans. Slim still dressed comfortably in light work clothes for his boiler-front Fireman/Water-tender Watch. The two made their way across the passageway from their quarters to the Mess for Mid-Watch rations …sandwiches, limeade "green bug juice" and sweet rolls.

Slim became a bit talkative as he ate and started telling Joey of his propensity to be easily distracted from completing routine chores he was embarked on. As an example, he told of leaving his wife without a word and shipping out on foreign articles after leaving his home; "… to buy a pack of cigarettes." Joey wanted the details behind this extraordinary and, in his opinion, somewhat demented move on Slim's part but he really didn't have the time for that explanation during this pre-watch, rations-break. He resolved to get the rest of the story later, during the trip to Korea.

During this mid-watch, Joey insured all the topside cargo handling machinery was kept hot and operating "in neutral gear setting", and ready to resume cargo handling with daylight. Joey knew that there would be little delay in starting the load-out, as overtime for the stevedores had been authorized! He also knew that daylight would see the Skipper concerned about *expediting the cargo load-out and if possible, completing it to allow the ship's departure from Beaumont that evening… for the Panama Canal Zone.* All that meant that, with daylight, there was to be cargo handling on a priority basis! *Nothing was to delay that effort!*

His rounds in the engine room were, likewise, being overseen by the ship's hierarchy. The Chief Engineer was on hand and he personally ensured the main engine was kept in a "ready to steam" condition. With the Chief on the Engine Room deck plates, again Joey wondered whether the on-watch Second Assistant Engineer had the trust of the Chief to stand his watch properly. Finally, with the mooring lines doubled, the ship test-ran the engine periodically. Joey thought the "big recip" ran beautifully. There were "no knocks" or "machinery squeals" (which would indicate excessive wear or a shortage of lubrication to any of its moving parts). His view of Slim at the boilers showed that Slim enjoyed a significant level of trust from his watch officer and the chief since he stood his watch "normally" and without any additional oversight.

The prior day's load out of the SS CHARLES MC GOWAN included Fresh & Frozen Stores (food stuffs) and that had the ship's day-working, Junior Engineer, checking out and then repairing a poorly running Consumable Stores Refrigeration System. It seems there had been refrigerant leakage from the system's Expansion Valve, and that led to abnormally higher "storage box temperatures".

On this, the second round of his afternoon watch, Joey saw the Junior Engineer working on the compressor-receiver section of the Stores Refrigeration Plant. This plant used the Freon 12 gas refrigerant versus the more commonly used ammonia gas refrigerant and Joey saw two Freon gas bottles standing close to the plant. Joey offered his assistance to the "Junior" for the repair; "If it wouldn't take too long… as I'm on watch and they'll be expecting me in the engine room soon." The Junior Engineer accepted his offer of help in checking for leaks following the repair and replacement of the plant's expansion valve and associated piping. Joey used the Halide (Acetylene-only torch set-up) that was handed to him to check for leaks in the rebuilt section. His check-sweep of the refrigeration plant disclosed no green flame from the torch; therefore no Freon 12 leaks. Joey was proud that he could offer assistance and be accepted to help in the repair. Smiling, he thought; "This is going to be a fine trip! Won't get to be boring if the rest of the "experienced" engineering team lets me participate in machinery repairs as they're needed."

Joey was correct in assuming nothing would stand in the way of the Skipper in his push for the earliest possible "underway time" for the ship. The rapid rice loading into the ship's cargo holds was an impressive thing for Joey to behold. The stevedores handled those sacks of rice on the dock and in the holds speedily and without any problems. Trucks with "more rice" kept arriving throughout the day...and were emptied promptly until the cargo holds were full. No time was wasted!

Joey spent his noon to 4 PM watch primarily insuring the cargo handling deck machinery operated seamlessly. This was a slightly abnormal focus for the Watch Oiler who usually concentrated on main engine and auxiliary machinery lubrication. While he still needed and subsequently obtained permission to concentrate on topside lube-needs, Joey was correct in assuming the Engineer on watch, the Second, on the engine room deck plates, would handle the minimal main engine lube-needs. This set-up allowed Joey to make his hourly rounds concentrating on lubricating the cargo handling, topside machinery. No matter what, overall attention to good engineering details was observed by both watch- standers!

In oiling the cargo handling gear, Joey was able to watch the cargo handling operation closely. He saw that when the last of the rice-carrying trucks was emptied, no time was lost prior to the arrival of other (ammunition carrying) trucks, with Army Military Police Detachments embarked. These latter arriving trucks held the ship's deck cargo of war fighting hardware to be carried to Korea. Again, virtually no time was wasted in transferring that gear (guns and ammunition) …and the two and a half ton trucks that carried the armaments, to the ship for stowage as deck cargo.

Following the completion of the deck cargo load out, the ship's Deck Department people, assisted by a few knowledgeable stevedores, covered, then battened down (with canvas coverings and canvas-tightening wooden wedges) the hatches to all cargo and ship's stores holds. With the exception of the "rolling-stock cargo" which was stowed (lashed down) on deck. At that point on the SS CHARLES MC GOWAN, all cargo was then made as "leak-proof" for the extended ocean voyage as was possible.

With an hour or so of daylight remaining when cargo operations ended, the Skipper had the word passed that the ship *would immediately get underway* from Beaumont and proceed to the Panama Canal to transit to the Pacific. Joey had wanted to go ashore in Beaumont to purchase some new steel-toed work shoes, but with the announcement, he put that "fanciful thought" behind him. In reflection, he was happy he had taken the time to say "his goodbyes" to Betty…but was a bit sorry he had neglected calling his mother and bidding her goodbye as well. He thought; 'Will get that done, along with, if possible, mailing a letter to her from the Panama Canal Zone'.

CHAPTER SIX

NEXT STOP; PANAMA

Previously, he had looked up the distance from Beaumont to the Canal and had come up with 1540 miles, give or take the mile or two that depended upon the "waiting anchorage" to be assigned to the Liberty by the Canal Zone authority. He knew that with the ship making the transit at her maximum speed of 11 knots, it would take four hours short of six full days to get there. In passing, he mentally compared the "normal steaming speed" of 17 knots made by the turbine-powered tank ships he had been sailing, with "getting somewhere over the horizon" on an "11-knot Liberty". The trip on the Liberty required a good measure of patience by everyone involved. Since Joey had no option, "patience" won out over irrationally wanting to; *"… make Panama by tomorrow morning"*.

Almost immediately upon taking departure from Beaumont the ship took a southerly heading that provided sufficient room for her to pass clear of the Yucatan Peninsula. Joey knew he'd be entering the tropics while passing Mexico so he "broke into" his sea bag to retrieve his lighter, "warm weather clothing". "Gonna now be able to give Slim a run for his money on dressing comfortably; he thought.

His watches, while steaming with a fully loaded-down reciprocating main engine, required Joey to fall back entirely on the "oiling instructions" given to him by Big Tom. He now routinely performed almost a full lube-round on the upper flats of the main engine while enroute the Operating Platform where he would relieve the 8 – 12 Watch Stander, Big Tom. Upon assuming the Watch he applied oil and water with the Flit Gun to cover the three engine-unit con-rod follower-guides. He then immediately took oil samples on his fingers from the three unit shaft journal and wrist pin bearing halves. Satisfied with the oil-sample findings that the engine was running (coolly and) as designed, he would report this to his Watch Officer.

His next "routine watch chore" was to request permission to and then check on the propeller shaft bearings and the stern tube stuffing box…both of which were aft of the Engine Room but were located on the lower engine deck level. Upon his return from the shaft alley to the operating platform, he would request permission to go topside aft and check the lubrication status and operation of the two steam-powered reciprocating Steering Engines (moving the ship's rudder)… and to check any other running deck machinery.

The "steering engine(s)" were the "Quadrant (drum) Type", and were directly connected to the tiller via the rudder post. These two small steam engines would alternate… with one backing-up the driving engine and the other, the "driving engine", providing power to the tiller-turning-rack-gearing. As with the other steam- engine-driven machinery, Joey's main lubricating tools for the steering gear were the cylinder oil and graphite grease pail and swab. Here also was a large covered pail of grease (for the pinion and screw gear racks) and a bin of rags for use in wiping up the slippery droppings that resulted from oilers using excess oil and grease. As he experienced in tankers, there was also an instruction sheet covered in clear plastic paper, noting the steps to take (in case of a power failure) for shifting the main steering station from the ship's bridge to the steering engine room… and for the power operation of the gear locally, and also locally, operation in the "hand mode". He noted that this Liberty ship had obviously been put into mothballs in an exceptionally clean condition, as the steering gear space "deviated from the filthy norm" he previously experienced. *There were no grease "droppings" on the ladder or deck areas of this Steering Engine Room!*

His lubrication-trips topside and to the Steering Engine were also important to his determination of the ship's "safe-steaming", and to satisfying his interest in the weather and how the "ship was riding". On this southbound leg of the voyage to Panama, the weather had been ideal and other than riding a long, low swell emanating from the Gulf of Mexico to the West, the "sea was flat". On each Noon–4 watch he checked with the Radio Operator, Sparks, a long time, professional seaman from WW II, who was routinely ensconced in his "radio-shack-home". While "the shack" could net some important upcoming ship's news, Joey's "check" was primarily for him to be updated on the weather forecasts for the remaining trip days. So far, all machinery had operated so well on the ship that if the weather "good fortune" continued, according to Sparks, they would be arriving at the Canal on time …as advertised! He knew this because the ship's (departing) "Beaumont to Panama Movement Report" to APL, told the operating company they would be arriving at the Canal about six days after leaving Beaumont.

Joey was happy about this relatively short transit prospect but by the third day, his time spent standing watches with a steaming reciprocating engine was beginning to "wear a bit thin" on him. The engine, operating at an unchanging 76 RPM, almost forced upon Joey and the other Engine and Fire-room room watch standers, a stupor, rendering them spellbound. The RPM beat-rate was insistent, and was close enough to their heart-beat rates that they actually adopted that rate for humming tunes or just plain thinking. Further adding to the discomfort, the further South the ship ran, the higher the engine room "heat sink temperature" grew to, as did the relative humidity the watch standers had to put up with.

CHAPTER SEVEN

THE PANAMA CANAL TRANSIT

The ship arrived on time at the anchorage at the Canal's designated "Atlantic waiting area"… for ships awaiting their turn for canal-passage to the Pacific. In Joey's eyes this arrival constituted the start of another "sea-going adventure". He was excited to be there in Colon, Panama. He had read up on the facts, and peculiarities to be encountered in a normal Canal, Atlantic to Pacific, passage, but he still wanted to be *topside to personally observe as much as was possible of the entire passage.* He also knew that "realistically", as a watch standing member of the engine room Black Gang, satisfaction of that "wish" was a bit farfetched.

Dropping the anchor in Panamanian waters in Limon Bay put the ship well within sight of Colon City, and also within sight of the Canal's "Atlantic entry point; the Gatun Locks", some 10 miles from the ship's anchorage. Joey knew that arrival at and entering that first set of Canal locks, the set of three Gatun Locks, would be the first real indication that the MC GOWAN was starting her "passage". In preparation for this passage start, the MC GOWAN Deck Department installed the steel holding-posts on the bridge wings, and to them fitted a sheet canvas awning. This action was taken to provide the shade needed for the comfort of the Canal pilots who would be standing on those bridge wings. A ready response to the question about this "pilot pampering" from Joey to one of the older AB's, let Joey know this shade-rigging was normal for ship's about to transit the Canal.

It was 10 AM when a large Pilot Boat arrived at the anchorage and made fast to the MCGOWAN starboard side directly at where the ship's wood step and manila line Jacob 's Ladder hung. In boarding and while still on the Jacob 's Ladder, the leading pilot hand-signaled the bridge to begin bringing the anchor back aboard. Also in the Pilot boat were some twenty to thirty Panamanian line handlers who, upon boarding the Liberty, divided their number into groups of three plus a leader and these groups immediately went to all the fore and aft ship's numbered line handling stations.

Upon their arrival, Joey, who was at his Maneuvering Station aft along with the Second Mate and the two #4 Line AB's, welcomed the Panamanian line handlers to the #4 Line Handling Station simply by shaking their hands. With Spanish being the primary language in Panama, the Panamanians had considerable trouble speaking with and understanding the American seamen...and vice versa. In his "welcoming the Panamanians" speech, the Second Mate advised the Americans aft that the Panamanians would "take the lead" in line-handling operations at the locks... and as needed during the transit. "Just do what they want us to do; *the Pilot will be talking to them!*" was the Second's "final guidance" to the ship's crew members. Having that much trust and faith in Panamanian line handling skills was strange to Joey and upon being so told by the Second Mate, his expression showed some surprise. The Mate, reading Joey's eyes, said: "Standard operating procedure in Canal transits!" That ended all debate on the subject.

The Panamanians worried little over the "Chain Of Command" employed in the MC GOWAN's handling of mooring lines...but did show considerable concern regarding their "own business dealings" with the American crewmembers. To a man, they all carried a white cloth sack, and in those sacks were scrimshaw-like carvings on wood, tightly rolled knotted rope hammocks, and some doilies made of much lighter, white cotton string. All this "artwork" was promoted for sale to the Americans by the Panamanians almost as soon as the latter arrived at the ship's mooring stations.

It was interesting to Joey that few transactions were consummated. At Station #4, only the Second Mate purchased anything and what he bought was a hammock. Regarding line handler comfort in the very hot Panamanian noon and early afternoon periods, Joey eased into the Engineering Mess and returned with a pitcher of iced water and half a dozen glasses on a tray. That water was well received and went along nicely with the Panamanians' lunches which were also ensconced in their white "barter sacks".

With the tug in an alongside "stand-by" mode and moving with the ship toward the first set of locks, Joey looked up to check the color of the stack smoke the MC GOWAN was making. Seeing the (desirable) light brown "economy haze", he thought; "We look professional! Good for Big Tom and the rest of the 8-12 Watch in the hole!"

Since this leg of the "Canal entry" was through relatively shallow water, Joey could feel the engine and propeller vibrations pulsating through the ship's main deck. Due to the slower ship's speed called for in that short transit, Joey observed; "For a change, the engine isn't turning at 76 RPM". Joey wondered what it's like to get "finger samples" of lube from the slower moving crankshaft. He knew he'd be finding that out long before this transit was over so he put the engine out of his mind and concentrated on the ship's approach to the Gatun Locks… noting the incredibly beautiful, distant mountainous and close-in, tropical low-land scenery.

Upon arrival at the first lock there was a pilot change. One of the pilots that had been picked up at the anchorage departed MC GOWAN via the tug boat. The tug departed for other business when the Panamanian line handlers "secured the ship in the lock". Prior to its leaving, the tug crew helped this "securing" by passing to the lock's pier-side line handlers (from both sides of the ship), the Heaving Lines with "21 Thread light rope lines" attached. The dock line handlers then hooked the "light rope lines" to much heavier "wire rope mooring lines"; each of these was terminated on the line-handling reels of both the port and starboard (two on each side of the lock) track-diesel towing machines.

These machines, while appearing to be not too large when viewed from the ship's deck, were each actually the size of a city bus and obviously, being composed of mostly a large, locomotive-sized engine, were very heavy. The "eyes" of the wire rope lines were then brought aboard the Liberty and fastened at the "forward and after, and both the port and starboard" ship's line stations. These dock side machines were known as (mechanical) "Mules" and the iron tracks they rode on, followed the sides of the lock and up to the loch doors; …where the Mules would go while pulling the Liberty ship into its final position in the lock.

The first lock had water in it at "Atlantic Ocean level" when the ship entered. Joey could see the high water level (discolored line) on the lock siding that would be the "high Lock water level" after adding water to raise the ship the required amount to sail the ship into the elevated second lock. In Joey's estimation, the ship would be lifted some 30 feet in this, the first of the Gatun Locks.

To Joey, for a man-made item, the lock looked huge since its dimensions were 110 feet wide by 1,050 feet in length. The Liberty, the MC GOWAN, by comparison was quite small. Its dimensions were only 57 feet in beam width and 441.5 feet in length, and so, if the Canal Authority so desired, two Liberty ships end-to-end could be moved through the individual locks at the same time. Joey looked forward past the bow on the port side and surprisingly, to him, there was a beautiful, wooden, two- mast, sailing vessel also positioned in the lock ahead of the Liberty. Like the Liberty, that vessel was also pointed up toward the second lock.

The four Mules affixed to the ship took over and started hauling the ship into position for flooding of the lock. Following in a "standing-by" mode, the tug continued with the Liberty into the lock, then departed when the lock operators were satisfied with MC GOWAN's position. The "ocean side" lock doors were then closed, and when they were shut, the flooding began…with a roaring vengeance! Joey, dumbfounded by the violence of the lock flooding, watched wide-eyed as the ship rose the 30 feet in some eight minutes!

When the flooding stopped, the MC GOWAN, rolling slightly from the turbulence, was readied to be moved into the second Gatun Lock. The Pacific-side lock door was then opened and the ship…and the schooner, as in the first lock, were again positioned in the second lock by Mules and readied for door closing and the lock flooding that was needed to raise the ship another 30 feet. With the same uproar as experienced in the first lock, the second lock was flooded and the MC GOWAN was raised an additional 30 feet. The procedure was repeated for the water level raise in the third and final Gatun Lock. The entire operation at the Gatun Locks took less than an hour and a half... and ended with the Liberty pointed directly into Gatun Lake.

The approximate 90 foot "total lift" of the transiting Liberty now had the ship at the same level as Gatun Lake ...and after unloading the Panamanian line handlers and Canal Lock Pilot to a lake-stationed tug boat, Gatun Lake was where the ship was now heading. The ship was now entirely under her own power and the engine "sounded sweet" to Joey. Her 76 RPM beat had him smiling...until the Bridge passed the word via the loud speaker system that the ship would be anchoring in Gatun Lake. The unexpected anchoring was the result of the Canal Authority deciding that it, the anchoring, "... was a prudent call". Rumor had it that a freighter making its way through the Pacific locks had a "slight collision problem" with the lock sidings and with one of that lock's doors. *That door would have to be replaced prior to any Canal transits being resumed.* At best, that repair job was estimated to take some five hours to complete. With some six transiting vessels being handled at various points in the Canal at any time, the Canal Authority thought it in the best interests of all that the MC GOWAN remain in the Lake anchorage until the situation cleared. Joey heard the anchorage assigned being referred to in a letter–number designation and immediately thought of the anchorages in New York Harbor being similarly identified.

It was shortly after noon when Anchoring Stations were relaxed for the crew. Because of manning his anchoring assignment, Joey had missed his normal lunch-start time of 11:15 AM... and needed to see the Watch "dogged" (shortened because of a specific and abnormal situation) in order to be relieved of the Oiler Watch and be able to take his lunch break. He was hungry and looked forward to the "light (tropics) lunch" of BLT sandwiches and fruit flavored "bug juice" but he had to wait until 1 PM to actually make it into the Mess. It all worked out to be just a minor irritation to Joey, but at the time, he worriedly thought he was going to miss a meal.

The ship anchored in Gatun Lake well clear of the locks but relatively close to the Atlantic-side entrance into the lake. The MC GOWAN was still anchored when Joey finished his Noon–4M Watch. Upon getting relieved, he went topside just to relax. His Watch rounds had taken him topside earlier and he had observed several Canal caiman (alligators) circling the MC GOWAN. He found that they, the caiman, had been in that mode since the ship had anchored. He got to the fantail just as two of the ship's cooks were preparing to dump some pork skins, fat and leg bone waste over the side. The cooks were accompanied by some of the younger members of the ship's company, for whom, like for Joey, this was their first Canal passage. Messmen, Ordinary Seamen, Wipers (and now Joey too) were watching the closer caimans for their reaction when the food waste hit the water. As expected, those caiman 'gators immediately went after the meat and bones that were dumped. There were some garbage-eating sea gulls in the vicinity as well, and they gave the gators "a run" for the smaller bits of meat floating about.

While aft and while "rubber-necking" the caiman feeding, Joey noticed several small, "one palm-tree" islands, relatively close to the anchorage, whose land surfaces were surrounded by sandy beaches and shallow, ski- blue water. These beautiful, tiny islands appeared to exist as boating destinations for vacationing Canal residents. With the large numbers of caiman in the immediate vicinity, Joey had a hard time understanding "… how anyone could seriously consider camping out here." He concluded with the thought; "Oh well, there is an awful "lot of stuff" that happens on this earth that I don't understand… and this is one of them." Later in the afternoon, the ship came to life with the passing of the word via the loud speaker system: "MAN THE ANCHOR DETAIL AND PREPARE TO GET UNDERWAY".

Anchor housed, the ship headed almost due South for a few miles then conformed to the standard track for leaving Colorado Island to the South while heading for the Canal's Gamboa Reach. While not overly slow, the ship's engine was again turning at a slower rate than its standard 76 RPM. The slower rate still had the ship doing some 6 knots toward the Gatun Locks. Joey could see the Gatun Dam further to the South and marveled at the engineering that went into the overall Canal construction about a half century earlier.

The Gamboa Reach followed several dramatic turns to conform to the Canal in its meandering toward the Pacific locks. The Reach was impressive in its own right with mountainous terrain to the Northeast and the distinctive signs of the engineering and cutting away of terrain involved in constructing this portion of the Canal. Joey spent as much time topside studying the Reach as was possible for him to do. He rationalized that he'd be able to catch up on needed rest and sleep "a plenty" after the transit… and while making for Hawaii in the Pacific. The Gamboa Reach was followed immediately by the Bas Obispo, Las Cascadas, Empire, Culebra, Cucaracha, Paraiso and Balboa Reaches. These were all close to each other and would be encountered on MC GOWAN's generally southeasterly track. In making this transit, Joey saw just how much digging had to be done to realize a "canal connecting the oceans" as an end-product. "Impressive!" was his mumbled appreciation for the Canal.

The Pedro Miguel (Miraflores) Locks, or the Canal's Pacific end-point, were the next and final hurdle for the Liberty ship. As like what happened for the Atlantic entry point, there was a tug boat standing by to help the Liberty enter the first lock. Again, Panamanian line handlers came aboard with the Lock Pilot and took their stations fore and aft and on both sides of the ship. There was a "replay" of the ballet played out on the Atlantic Canal-end by the Mules in positioning MC GOWAN in the first, the highest, of the Pedro-Miguel locks. This time the Liberty was alone in the lock…no sailing schooner or any other craft was on hand to make this portion of the transit with her. Also, this lock had the Liberty enter the lock at the high water, or the "Lake Level" water height. The ship had to be lowered some 90 feet to be at the Pacific Ocean level.

This first lock would lower her 1/3 of the way. This time Joey watched as the ship dropped the 30 feet in eight minutes! There were no cascading and noisy water level changes as was noted in the Atlantic locks. The water from the first lock was simply drained into the second lock, to allow the Liberty to be easily moved into. As that lock did its "lowering job" there was another tug standing by to help the ship through Miraflores Lake and then into to its last locks, the Pacific or Miraflores Locks.

The 90 foot downward lock-excursion completed, the Liberty unloaded the Line handlers and Canal Pilots and took onboard the Gulf of Panama and Pacific Ocean-Canal Slot Pilots. Transiting the Gulf of Panama and the handling of Pilot Boat and offloading of the last of the pilots went by in about an hour… and then the ship took departure from Panama, and made for Oahu, Hawaii.

CHAPTER EIGHT

GOING TO HAWAII

The Great Circle route from Panama to Oahu was quite long in itself; being about 5717 miles...or, at the speed of the Liberty, a run projected to take almost twenty two days to complete! The first leg of that Great Circle route took the MC GOWAN northwest and very close to the Pacific Coast of Costa Rica and the rich, game fishing grounds off the Gulf of Panama and Costa Rica. Joey did see the charter fishing vessels working the coastal waters and they were of virtually "all shapes and sizes", and there was a large population of them.

Nightfall came and with it a bit of a sea breeze was felt going eastward, against the ship's motion, and ending ashore in Central America. The next day came with a blazing sun and with the ocean and climate, "calm". Just the ocean swell lifting the ship, gave those onboard sensitive enough to feel it, the sense of their movement through the sea. All aboard did feel the main engine vibrations and were reassured by this, knowing they were going "somewhere" in this absence of life, and desert-like, but wet world of the Pacific's tropical ocean. The Liberty was again doing 11 knots with the engine running at her steaming speed of 76 RPM; and she was on her Great Circle heading, generally northwest on this, the first leg of the track to Oahu.

Joey's night Mid-watch went well. He concentrated on the lubrication of the main engine, shaft alley and the engine room machinery. His topside hourly watch-round found him looking in on the Steering

Engine and noting the satisfactory rudder operation. He had no reason to go forward on deck since all cargo handling machinery was "asleep when at sea", but he did note the ship's sides and small bow wave as the Liberty moved through the water. On this, a moon-less night, the stars shone brightly and there was the occasional slap of a flying fish hitting the hull or the metal siding of the house of the ship. He again wondered whether these flying fish would make a tasty breakfast if fried and served like trout. He resolved to find the answer to this question before this voyage to Korea was over.

Joey fell into "daily routines". For example; following the Mid Watch and a few hours of sleep daily, he was up for breakfast at 7 AM. He enjoyed the fresh fruit that was served and also ate (his routine); eggs over-medium, crispy bacon and toasted white bread. He missed his morning bagel but all the bagels had been eaten and while the cooks were proficient in baking white bread, none had been to "bagel-baking school". He also enjoyed conversing with shipmates whenever possible. For example, while alone on the second day of the transit, after breakfast, Joey smoked his Camel on the deck outside and to port of the mid-ships house while he sized up his work clothes requirements from here in the tropical sea to Oahu. He resolved that the stuff he would wear would be exceptionally light, and be comprised of; his light cotton, and cut-down, short pant-Jeans, short sleeve (Jean) shirts and light socks. He was already wearing most of these items with this, his breakfast outfit this morning.

As Joey smoked, Slim came outside the House for his smoke, and the two then talked about the marvels they had seen during the Canal transit. Slim made the comment; "…mah fren's fum down in de Texas swamp 'ud never believe me if'n ah tol' dem 'bout it…". Joey responded with; "… my city-boy buddies'd need a little convincing too. I honestly think me telling them about the 'gators would get me called a "stretcher-of-the-truth"…as a bare minimum!" Slim nodded to this statement and the two roommates finished their smokes in silence. Neither Joey nor Slim wanted to go back to bed and sleep anymore. Joey then asked Slim to finish his; "…goin' out fo' cigarettes and didn't get back home fo' several months…" story.

Slim got that now familiar, slight smile on his face and with his best Texas accent, dove into telling the story. "Really wouldn't be much of a story. Jest needed a smoke an' our carton of butts was empty. Think de wife was workin' on our dinna when I went to de drug sto' onna corner fo' mo' smokes. Anyhow…don' recall getting' de smokes…jest remember getting' to de Houston hirin' hall an' askin' de dispatcher iff'n he had *any ship goin' anywhere* that needed an engineerin' ratin'. Da dispatcher said; "Yep, dere's a tanka at de wharf in Galveston Bay lookin' fo' a Fireman…an' ah'll give yo a lift in mah cah to da Bay Sea Taxis to catch her…iff'n yo' wan' it. He gave me de lift an' ah signed onta dat tanka. Don' know wha' ah did it dat-a-way to dis day,…but dat's wha' ah did. Thank mah wife wen out-a-her-haide wif worry when ah didn' come-on back home dat night. Ya know? When ah realized wha' ah'd dun, ah called her fum da ship wit da skipper's OK…an' apologized. She jest thanked me for de call … an' mah plan to get her a monthly allotmen'… an tol' me to come-on-home after ahm dun wif da tanka'. Grai' gal!"

Joey just shook his head with wonder at the conclusion of Slim's story. Jokingly he told Slim; "I'm gonna keep my eyes on you during our first liberty off the ship. I'm getting kind of used to you as my roomie and would miss you if you disappeared on me like you did on your wife back in Houston. By the way, the skipper has all the smokes you'd ever need, in his slop chest…an' if you run out of money to buy those smokes, I'll back you for a carton or two." Slim had a broad smile on his face after Joey's last comment. He mumbled something like; " Happy y'all don' thank ahm a nut or sumpin'…". Joey just laughed.

A flying fish picked that exact moment to hit the side of the House and land almost at Slim's feet. Joey picked up the wet, foot long, now eyeless and dead fish and headed back inside the house to the engineering mess. He went up to the Mess' cook and asked if that fish could be cooked up for him. The cook said; "Sure. But you probably won't like it. I hear tell the meat is stringy an' kind a' dry. Also, it'll probably take three or so of 'em to make you a decent meal. An' I'd cook them like I'd cook a trout, but probably with a little extra butter in the pan." Joey thanked him with; "No thanks.", and did not press the issue of having a mess of these flying fish cooked for him.

Joey and Slim went back into their quarters and Slim hit his bunk to catch some shut-eye while Joey sat at the room-desk to write a letter to his Mom. The words for the letter did not come easily. He was fifteen minutes into it and still had not mentioned shipping out on this ship, his first Liberty ship, "knowing" Betty in Beaumont, the Canal transit… and just what his "Oiler" work consisted of. He excused himself with thinking that; "… I'm not in the mood to write home just yet, but I will get it done before we arrive in Hawaii!" Pushing himself away from the desk he thought it inordinately "warm and sticky" here in the quarters. Since they were definitely in the tropics, he started topside to adjust the air duct ventillator scoops to insure that any of that "relative wind up on the roof" would go to the berthing spaces in the mid-ships house.

Upon arrival topside he saw there was little adjustment needed for the scoops. Thinking; 'Maybe a cool shower is the answer to this ungodly tropical heat.' He then stripped off his shirt and under shirt. Bare from the waist up and with the small portable fan running, he began to feel some comfort from the now considerable forced-air-motion in his quarters. After removing his shoes he climbed up into his bunk to get some rest…if sleeping was possible. He found; it was still not possible! He then just went topside thinking; "I'll eventually get just plain tired enough to go to sleep…heat or no heat."

The tropical-variety, moist-heat didn't let up for the better part of a week of the three week transit to Honolulu. Joey and almost the entire crew became more adept at catching their sleep by getting clear of the overly warm quarters and hauling their mattresses, sheets and pillows (bedding) topside nightly. No one in authority tried to stop this practice, hence all on board caught up on their sleep "under the stars".

Into the fifth day of the Canal to Oahu nominal 22 day transit for the Liberty, the ship left the super-uncomfortable tropical environment and on taking a slight Northwesterly leg of the Great Circle track, started picking up the prevailing Westerly winds. With a 15 knot relative wind now coming at the ship head-on, the MC GOWAN became downright comfortable! Gone were the "generally rampant bitching (complaining) and statements of misery" that had been coming from the crew. Appetites returned as did smiles and the conversation-enhancing "sea stories". While still a couple of weeks away, people were excitedly talking about what they'd be doing on their Hawaiian liberty. Joey was no exception to this and openly spoke about seeing what was in the Hawaiian offering as relates to young, beautiful and... willing women. Slim, who had "heard it all" before from Joey, just smiled and said he had not been away from his wife that long that he; "...had to be on the hunt". Joey came back with; "Glad I ain't got no wife!"

About the only "hitch in her giddy-up" that the main engine showed was that the higher (in the vicinity of 80 degrees Fahrenheit) sea water "injection temperature" experienced in the tropical latitudes,...and with that, the higher ambient running temperatures that became the norm for the engine. Joey had this situation in mind during all of his Oiler Watches. *He spent extra time insuring that nothing except the steamy interior of the engine's cylinders, ran "hot".*

The Second Assistant Engineer also was a worrier, and would occasionally double check the engine's lubrication status immediately following Joey's rounds. While that much concern was a bit "over the top", the ship actually benefitted from this "loving care". There had been no major machinery or equipage break downs (to date) and all aboard had settled into the "steady-steaming" routine. The older, more experienced engineering crew members had nothing but praise for the MC GOWAN. "The guys that put this bucket into mothballs following WW II, all rate being awarded medals. Never heard of a tropical transit going problem-free...but we're doing it!" In various spoken forms, this was a popular exclamation.

Once the prevailing Westerly winds became the norm, he found "the shade" in his quarters to be his most comfortable hang-out. He didn't care for those watch- mandated "trips topside" made by him during this portion of the transit since they were primarily made to check on the status of the Steering Engine... which ran beautifully. Also, topside "smokes" after the meals were a necessity to Joey and these became really the only times he and Slim got together and just..."shot the shit" (talked). If he was in the quarters, Slim slept! Joey needed conversations, so he braved the tropical heat to make these talks happen.

Further, with his watch standing in the "routine" category and with a lack of hardware repairs to be done, Joey almost couldn't get used to the resulting "lazy environment". He knew he'd have to wait for the day prior to the ship's arrival in Oahu to bring the cargo and anchor handling topside machinery "back to life", and he couldn't wait for that day to arrive. He did not however, permit himself to be overly bored. One of the ploys he used to keep his alertness up was by listening to music...even if the music was generated by him. He loved music and he was not unhappy with his (the 76 RPM engine beat-induced) humming of songs. He thought Western music lent itself to the engine's beating better than did other music types. Hank Williams' stuff was Joey's favorite music and the occasional pick-up of radio from the over-powered stations in Clint or Del Rio, Texas, had Williams', at times "teary ballads" in the airways a-plenty.

As the ship climbed into more northerly latitudes, the ambient temperature continued to drop. Being in a good mood and enjoying cooler temperatures worked out well for Joey. He finished his letter to his mom. He did extra "system tracing" in the engine room to better understand the operation of the ship's entire engineering plant, and he started working with the day-working specialists; the ship's Machinist, its Electrician and its Junior Engineer. All the resulting work came to pass after Joey obtained the Second's "blessing"; because, after all, the Second was Joey's immediate boss and could have hoarded Joey's day-working efforts. Joey's basic system- understanding and the professional checking of the refrigeration plants (for example) became almost "easy" to him under the tutelage of these same "experts"... and he became an exceptionally busy and knowledgeable worker with these people when "off watch". They in turn, thought the world of Joey! The net result of his efforts was; he was able to experience the best of all shipboard-working worlds: enjoy his work, and be appreciated for its accomplishment.

Joey now shifted his non-working, off-watch attention to learning as much as he could about the Territory of Hawaii, and more specifically about where he was to visit; the city of Honolulu on the Island of Oahu.

He knew the Great Circle Track laid out for the ship would bring it north of Molokai, with the "Big Island", Hawaii, further to the south. Both islands would be close enough to be seen from the ship, and as luck and climate would have it and with no main engine break-downs, be seen in the early morning of the arrival day. "Just be patient!" he told himself. "Only the greater part of a day left before we see and walk on Oahu. Gonna be fun!"

CHAPTER NINE

HAWAII; FINALLY!

Sure enough, after his Mid to Four AM watch, while "manning the port railing" with Slim, in anticipation of their arrival in Hawaii, Joey saw the lights on Maui to the South. He couldn't wait for dawn to shed enough light on these "island treasures" so he could really see them in detail. Slim was also excited about going to Hawaii but, compared to Joey, he was positively "laid back"!

At this time, following their final Watch prior to arriving at West Loch in Pearl Lagoon on Oahu, a relatively loud and smiling Slim held forth to Joey that; "Ah'm agonna hit Waikiki Beach so ha'd, de locals a'gonna thank a tropical storm is on 'em." Joey came back with a laugh and; "Gonna go ashore an' just get a carton of ciggy-butts?" It was now Slim's turn to laugh… Both seamen stayed awake through the breaking of dawn, and they stayed topside… and were the first people at the table for breakfast.

The day workers and the 8 to 12 Watch went to work immediately following breakfast with only 110 nautical miles remaining for the ship to transit westerly prior to its arrival at the Sea Buoy, "PH", marking the entrance to Pearl Harbor. The 110 nm trip would take a nominal 10 hours and put the ship in the Pearl Harbor Ship Channel about mid afternoon; …maybe early enough to happen while Joey was still on his Noon to Four PM watch. No matter what, Joey knew there'd be a call to man the Anchor Detail prior to the pilot's arrival to guide the ship into Pearl Harbor's West Loch. Happily, with his Anchor Detail Station being topside and aft, he knew he'd be able to see virtually all of the "ship's entry into and through Pearl Lagoon".

Joey's thoughts on what would happen when the ship arrived at the sea buoy were right on. The crew was called to anchor/mooring stations and then the ship took the pilot on board. The tug that the pilot arrived on fell in astern and trailed the MC GOWAN into the "PH Main Ship Channel".

The track into Pearl Harbor left the commercial harbor for Honolulu far to the east and actually made for the PH Harbor entrance on a northern leg, leaving military air bases on both the eastern and western shores. The area had a distinctive flowery scent and was a "tropical paradise treat" for eyes that have spent the past several weeks at sea staring at that "wet desert". Entering Pearl Harbor one viewed abundant foliage all around. Hanging onto the wire lifeline, because of the crystal-clear water, Joey was positive he could see the reef the ship passed over and through as it transited the harbor entrance. The ship made landfall in Pearl Lagoon with Hickam Army Air Base abeam to starboard and Cubi Point Naval Air Station to port, and then passed (the Naval) "Hospital Point" to starboard and continued up the ship channel until it arrived at the channel entrance to West Loch and the ammunition loading area contained therein. All of this latter transit was toward the western segment of the Harbor and terminated physically close to Pearl City, Oahu.

Making way up West Loch was an "interesting" transit. There were railroad tracks leading up the Loch and on the Northern shore there were two barge wreck residues. The keel iron from these barges rested on the north shore like two blankets. Joey asked one of the #4 Line AB's who had been to West Loch during WW II if he knew anything about the keels and how they came to rest where they were. The AB responded with; "They've been where they are since the war. Seems the ammo loading team for those barges was working aviation-carried ordinance… and think it was a carrier load-out of 100 lb bombs for attack aircraft. Don't know whether it was an inadvertent spark or what that set off some leaking explosive powder-charge from one of the bombs, but once that "leaker" went off, most of the rest followed suit. Think a whole bunch of Negro stevedore-ammo-handlers went up with the fireworks 'cause there was a sit-down strike following the blast. Think that carrier was delayed on deploying for a few days to a week 'cause of that strike. Anyway, the Navy here at the Ammo Piers likes to point at those keels to make their "safety briefing points". By the way, we'll be mooring well up in the Loch almost in Pearl City; ...great liberty there!"

Joey had heard that Pearl City's major "fun spot", the Pearl City Tavern, was within walking distance of the West Lock (PC) Gate... and the MC GOWAN's mooring spot. He had mentally put Pearl City down as the desirable "liberty spot" for his first night in the Islands.

The mooring went problem-free and with just a slight nudge from the tug to buck the tidal flow. Here in the upper reaches of West Loch, the only item to be planned for was the diurnal tidal surge. By chance, the Liberty moored when the tide was pretty close to high water, so the expected tidal flow was out to sea and that would further slacken the mooring lines...then the tide would come back in for the next 11 or so hours. Other than because of some cargo handling, that mooring situation with slackening then tightening mooring lines made the major point of interest (and for line tension readjustments) for the mates and deck seamen on watch during the ship's stay there.

Without further ado a self propelled fuel barge made up alongside to starboard. Joey, along with the Second Assistant, lined up the fueling manifold to receive "a big drink" of heated "Bunker C". This fueling was handled easily by the two of them.

Joey was hungry. Being on his station for anchoring and mooring, Joey had missed his noon meal. He knew he'd be able to catch up on eating when he was on liberty...so put that concern out of his mind. He had also missed the "laying up" of the Main Engine for the in-port stay. He thought hopefully; "There'll be plenty of opportunities for adding that evolution to his experience level in the future." But he was concerned that port visits came and went without his putting the "Reciprocating Beast" to sleep.

Earlier this day, when he was on the After Deck for the Maneuvering Watch he was in position to make the "after cargo and stores winches" ready to handle the expected additions to MC GOWAN's deck cargo and stores and also to replenish the now seriously depleted fresh and frozen food stuffs. This he did. The Deck Seamen and Steward's Department people appreciated Joey's fore-thought, caring and help.

All those load-outs happened without fuss! Four PM came and upon being relieved, Joey left the after and mid-ship deck areas... and immediately shifted into comfortable and clean shore-going clothes. Since the Second Assistant Engineer was still below in the plant, Joey dropped down to the operating level and requested permission of the man to go ashore. The Second gave Joey a "thumbs-up" on the liberty request, and called up to him that they'd probably see each other ashore later on.

CHAPTER TEN

A PEARL CITY LIBERTY

Joey's trip down the gangway was done at a trot. He found himself talking to the (Pearl City-West Loch) Gate Guard only minutes later. The guard confirmed that the Pearl City Tavern usually became the night-time gathering place for the locally residing Japanese "War Brides" (...among other ladies). These were ladies that had been married to GI's, and then imported from Japan into Hawaii by those same GI's, all who had been stationed in Japan since WW II ended. What that meant to Joey was that these ladies were probably just a few years older than he was, and if available, were experienced at extra-marital (and undetected) romantic escapades. 'No problem!' he thought. Answers to a couple of more questions directed by Joey to the gate guard led Joey to believe that the husbands of the ladies he'd meet, were probably working the night shift at the Pearl Harbor Naval Base.

Joey actually arrived at the Pearl City Tavern (PCT) at about 5 PM... during what he euphemistically called "amateur hour". Since he hadn't eaten on the ship prior to his leaving it, he was quite hungry so "dining at the PCT" took his thoughts upon entry, ...and after all, the place was a Chinese-American restaurant! After checking out the empty (of people) Monkey Bar area that the place was famous for, he found a small restaurant table close to the monkeys and helped himself to a menu. He noted that the early hour caused the PCT wait-staff to basically ignore 5:30 PM diners in favor of enjoying private conversations amongst themselves. Joey was close to formally complaining about the lack of service when, in strolled Slim.

Slim was having problems seeing in the relatively dark PCT after coming in from a super-bright "low-hanging sun-lit" stroll from the PC Gate. He blinked and rubbed his eyes continuously for what seemed to Joey to be over a minute. Joey saw that Slim looked dapper. He had donned a quite flowery and colorful, loose fitting short sleeve shirt hanging over a pair of hip-hugging khaki pants that, in turn were hanging out over a pair of leather thong sandals…sans socks. Knowing that Slim still had not distinguished Joey from other objects in the dark interior of the bar-restaurant, Joey called out to him and invited him to sit at the table with him.

It took Slim two tries to finally make out his roommate…and then approached smiling broadly and sat down…his back to the entrance and inquired; "We inna cave? Darker'n hell in here!" Joey's response was a matter of fact; "Seamen oughta know better than to stare at the setting sun. How come you forgot that? Besides, those stupid monkeys like it dark in here, and management is trying to keep them happy." Slim let Joey know; "Ah'll be damned if'n ah'm agonna pull a liberty wif some damned monkeys. Jest came in here to see y'all an' let ya know ahm aheadin' to Waikiki. Missus'd never fo'give me iff'n ah came alla'way to Hawaii and missed seeing Waikiki. Besides… gotta get'er some souveneirs.. fo' sho'!" Joey couldn't let the tongue-in-cheek opportunity to slip by without again warning Slim to stay away from those "memory-affecting" cigarette purchases. "Sure hate to break-in a new roomie for the rest of the trip to Korea. Got kind of used to you…" was the wind-up comment in that regard.

Joey asked Slim if he wanted to eat here with him at the PCT prior to leaving for the beach area. Slim, wiser than he acted, came back with; "Two dranks an' ah'll be a- fo'getting all abou' Wahkiki. Ah'll be a-eatin' when ah gets dere. Think fo' now, ah'l jest jump inta one-a those taxis awaitin' outside… an' see y'al d'next time on de mid-watch."

A smiling Joey wished Slim a great evening as his roommate pushed his chair back and started for the door. Just prior to Slim leaving the table, a pair of deck seamen off the ship had slid into the "monkey bar end" of the bar and had overheard Slim and Joey's parting words. As Slim passed them, one of the seamen let him know they were also going to Waikiki …and asked if Slim wanted to split the cost of the taxi ride there with them. Slim readily agreed and the three of them left the PCT together. Joey didn't really know why, but he was pleased Slim wasn't going Waikiki-bar-hopping on his own.

Slim's departure was almost immediately followed by the arrival of the Second Assistant Engineer. Joey put formality aside and called out to his squinting and eye-rubbing watch mate; "Hey Second! Why don't ya come on over. Seems we're both a bit early. I was going to get a bite of some Chinese food now, right here at the PCT. Wanna join me?" The Second wasted no time in joining Joey and as he pulled up his chair asked what Joey had ordered. Joey responded; "Nothing yet but I was looking at a dish of Szechwan Beef, fried rice and egg roll… and also maybe some egg-drop soup with hard noodles." The Second, checking Joey's menu mumbled that Joey's choices sounded; "… good, but think I'll stick with chicken…an' in here they got a hot variety that's also in the *Szechwan category.*" The Second joined Joey in trying to get the attention of the (totally ignoring them) wait-staff. He didn't make out any better than Joey did with trying to get their attention using normal arm waving. Not believing the situation, the Second mumbled to Joey; "*We got "BO", or what?* " With that he stood and approached the chattering bevy of ladies on the wait-staff. His entre' "stage whisper" and movement toward them definitely got their attention. The food the two seamen ordered was on the table within minutes.

"Looking at monkeys" aside, their "Chinese dinner" tasted just as it was expected by them to taste; like good (American) food with Chinese names, served in a "Chinese" restaurant. "This chow is great!" the Second opinioned. "Should hold us over for the night…and I hope I don't burp up all that garlic when I'm romancing some gal a little later on." Joey nodded and added; "You know about the Japanese "war brides" that're supposed to hang out here starting at sunset …?" The Second came back with; "Not formally on this trip, but the place is famous for treating seamen such as us, very well! I'm assuming female companionship goes along with that "treatment". Japanese, Nisei,

Kanaka or whatever, some lady's gonna do just beautifully with me tonight! By the way, *what else have* you *"heard"?"*

While Joey was recounting what the Pearl Harbor gate guard had told him concerning the Japanese "War Brides" hitting the PCT at about sunset, the two watch mates were laid-back while drinking their Budweiser beers …and weren't really aware of how much daylight was left. They weren't the only seamen off the Liberty ship in the bar but they were ignored by the others (a couple of the Mates off the ship) and they, in turn, ignored those "Mate Deck Apes".

They did not have to wait too long. Two thin, smallish, black haired ladies arrived and did not appear to suffer from "setting-sun blindness". These ladies both wore loose fitting, peasant blouses and plaited, brownish knee length skirts. They weren't wearing uniforms, per se, but they did appear quite similar in their look-alike outfits. Because of their diminutive size they reminded Joey of a small, thin and pretty Jewish girl of his age, named Ruby, who lived on his block in Coney Island. He had thought many times of "taking her out" when they were seniors in high school but never did. Shortly after this "unrequited love" scenario with Ruby, he "fell hard for" another classmate, Ellie Massimino.

The Second wasted no time in hailing the ladies and inviting them to join Joey and him…and have something to drink. To bring the point home, he noisily dragged the two extra chairs into place at the table and quite chivalrously, with a wave of his arm and a slight bow, gestured for the Asian ladies to join them. That's all it took for the two seamen to be paired up for the night with local ladies "on the prowl", at the PCT.

Upon the group taking their seats, introductions were completed and Joey found out his "girl -friend's" name was Tomiko and the lady the Second "latched on to" was Sachiko. They were Japanese nationals who were brought into Hawaii by soldiers they had met and married in Japan. Their husbands were now employed by the Federal Government and now worked for the US Navy at West Loch in Pearl Harbor. The ladies choice of drink was "whiskey and water over ice" in tall glasses.

Within minutes, the seamen determined the ladies were, quite literally, "tea-totelers" as tea had been used to insure the "realistic coloring" of the drinks. While they did not openly work for the PCT, by prior agreement with the place's management, they drank non-alcoholic drinks with "their dates" while the restaurant charged the price a real drink was going for. This wasn't the first time either the Second or Joey had been with "bar girls" that played their companions for "fake drinks" on the bar's behalf. They knew that this practice also insured the girls would not get drunk as the evening wore on. Neither man was troubled by the ploy. They believed this "drink buying" was just what they had been working for, and what they were paid to buy.

The couples got to know each other better with the passage of the time it took the band to get set up for entertaining the PCT customers. The English spoken by the girls was somewhat stilted and they did have the problem with pronouncing "l's"... that came out "r's". Native Japanese were known to suffer from this defect in their verbal handling of English. "Pronunciation" aside, these girls had absolutely no problem with their understanding of the English language as spoken by the two seamen.

The PCT's Hawaiian "Aloha Band" was now playing and their first choice for music was a Hawaiian Chant... The "Polynesian chants", as such, were not really conducive to being danced to. The chant was well done however, and was accompanied by a lit-torch-wielding Hawaiian male dancer. The music and the dance were well received and the now crowded restaurant-bar area erupted loudly in vocal and hand-clapping applause. Both Tomiko and Sachiko were smilingly convincing each other that the performance was "...joto des'u!", or "...well done!"

The Second wasted little time in inviting Sachiko to depart the PCT for her "more comfortable digs", which he did "with class". On hearing this, Joey immediately suggested to his watch partner that they plan on meeting back here at the PCT at about 11: 15 PM so that they could make their requirement of "watch relief time", on the ship, at 11: 45 PM. The Second and Sachiko left at almost the exact time the Hawaiian chant tune was completed. Joey opted to stay at the PCT a while longer and do a bit of dancing with Tomiko.

The next tune the band did was an American variety of a; "... slowish two-step". Joey asked Tomiko to dance and she "helped in moving along their romantic inclinations" by holding Joey as close as possible as they danced. The dancing, after so much time at sea, rejuvenated him. He happily danced with his eyes closed and it occurred to him that in all the time he spent with Betty in Beaumont, that time never included tender moments like this; which just entailed doing some affectionate slow-dancing. Slow and close dancing with Tomiko made Joey very happy, indeed!

It was Tomiko that suggested they leave the PCT for her place. With a turn of her head to indicate the direction they would take, Tomiko said in accented Pigeon English "…wight up brock on Karakawa. Thwee minute walk. You gonna rike!" Joey squared up with the PCT on the bill, a bill that also included the cost of the Second's dinner and drinks. Joey didn't give the situation of being monetarily "taken" by the Second a second thought. He knew the Second would be "good for squaring away" on "the money thing" with him; …and would be very prompt in complete, and at first opportunity, payment.

Their chairs made a bit of a squeaking noise with the floor on being pushed back. The squeaks got the attention of the folks at neighboring tables. Other than those flickering glances, nobody really paid any attention to their leaving. Joey pondered this "lack of concern" a bit thinking these "war brides" must have a local reputation for picking up and then leaving the PCT with seamen. "Good for me…!" he thought.

Tomiko was accurate. Just one short block away was a "single-wall thickness", wooden-sided and quite plain house that sported a three-step set of stairs leading up to the front door. "Dees my prace…" she said while reaching into her tiny purse for the key. It was hard for Joey to believe but here it was about 8 PM, it still wasn't fully dark outside,… and he was already being invited into a lady's home, most assuredly for some love-making. He laughingly thought; "Just good Ol' Hawaiian hospitality …and, "Praise The Lord", let's waste no time in making it all happen."

The entry room was warmly lighted as there was a small table lamp that had been left lit during the period Tomiko had left for the PCT and been gone. The lamp was located on an end table near a white, black and brown, plaid-colored lounge, where it helped bring out the color in that relatively drab furniture item. With all the window shades pulled shut, this one, small lamp surprisingly gave the entire front room, or Living Room, a very warm feeling.

Leading off the Living Room to the left was a small kitchen (really, just a kitchenette), and a bedroom and bathroom to the right. In realtor's terms the home would be described as a: "…nicely maintained, unassuming, delightful, one bedroom-one bath, *starter home,* and very conveniently located in Pearl City,… on the main Oahu bus route,… and a steal at… (whatever amount that sort of real estate was going for at the time)".

Upon entry, Tomiko went directly to the kitchenette, and opened a cabinet over the sink that contained two quart bottles of liquor; …a bottle of gin and one of Canadian whiskey. With a single wave of her arm she "asked" Joey if he wanted a drink…, and if so, out of which bottle. Knowing that her husband probably knew, quite precisely, how much liquor was in the two bottles, Joey responded that he'd had enough to drink at the PCT. *"Joto!"* (Good!)… was her pleased response. She closed the cabinet and headed to a 78 RPM record player. The record in position to be played contained some very good dance music by Benny Goodman.

With the music start, Tomiko held out her arms for Joey to move into, when he chose to dance. He couldn't refuse her invitation and they danced to two numbers prior to stopping. Tomiko was enjoying the dancing immensely…and didn't want to stop…but did when she felt Joey's erection. She held onto Joey's hand and led him into the bedroom.

With a slight tug of her arm, Joey turned her to face him and along with a tight embrace, kissed her fully on her slightly parted lips. Arching her back and with even stronger urgency, she pressed herself into his body with the kiss. Holding her very closely, Joey responded by sliding his hand down her back and fondling her. With enhanced passion, Tomiko started undoing Joey's shirt, then went to his belt and fumbled with undoing his trousers. With his shirt gone, Joey did not release her from the hug and continued to caress her and also continued undressing by stepping out of his shoes, trousers and under draws. He then gently picked her up and, carrying her as he would a bride "across the thresh hold", he softly placed her on the bed.

They made love passionately. Joey had never made love to an Asian girl and was surprised at Tomiko's physical flexibility and body control. In a way, he envied her husband. When they finally relaxed into the bed fully satiated, Joey made the comment: "Tomiko...I wish this evening would never end...but you know that I've got to be back aboard my ship tonight,... and that means I've got to leave here no later than 11 o'clock. I haven't told you before but I'm fairly certain I'll be leaving West Loch tomorrow. That means, with getting the ship ready to go, my day tomorrow will not allow any more shore leave...so I won't be seeing you again...unless we stop back here in Hawaii when our Korean deliveries are finished."

She held her hand to his lips to stop his rhetoric, slid out of bed and from the dresser, grasped a hand sized, Shinto-temple-gate-shaped thing with gong, black lacquer painted Japanese icon, and presented it to him. "Dees a Torii. Keep it near you bed on ship an' eet breeng good ruck." By this time, Joey had learned a couple of Japanese conversational phrases, and smilingly responded with; "Arrigato, Tomiko." (...Thank you, Tomiko.) She just said: "Hai" (Yes.), and changed the subject. "Hope you come back. You good man! I rike! Prease remember me."

Instead of dressing and with still a half hour to go before he had to leave, Joey allowed as how; "Think I will have that drink now. Please make it whiskey". Naked, she wheeled into the kitchenette, got ice from the refrigerator freezer into a water glass and poured a touch of water into it. After retrieving the whiskey, she passed the drink-makings to Joey for him to do the pouring...which he did, making a very light "high ball" drink. Instead of immediately drinking from the glass, Joey offered it to Tomiko. She declined saying; "Husband come home soon. He smer. No good!" Joey sipped from the glass and then pulled Tomiko back and close to him. He again kissed her with passion...she again returned the passion. They just nakedly lay there in the bed. Both were happy for having this evening.

Fully dressed and ready for his meeting with the Second, Joey kissed Tomiko good-bye and departed her house for the PCT. He was on time and wondered if the Second would be late, and he reflected that he didn't know where the Second had spent the evening, so if he missed their meeting time, finding him would be a chore and would probably mean he would have to return to Tomiko for her friend's address and directions on how to get there. He turned to check up Kalakawa Avenue in the dark and was pleasantly surprised to see the Second striding toward him from the same direction as where Tomiko's house was located.

"Hi Joey"; the Second called. "Seems like we're gonna make the ship in time for our Watch after all. Have a good time tonight?" "Damn right!" Joey shot back with a smile. "Gonna remember Pearl City 'till we get to Pusan…and maybe even longer." Almost in lock step they strode down to the Pearl Harbor, "PC" Gate and the SS MC GOWAN.

CHAPTER ELEVEN

THE TRIP RESUMES

It was on Joey's Noon to 4 PM Watch that the remainder of the additional deck cargo had been loaded and the ship completed replenishment of all consumables. At about 3: 30 PM, and with the Maneuvering Watch Stations manned, a single Navy tug was made fast astern, and with the retrieval by the Liberty ship of her mooring lines, the tug pulled the MC CORMACK clear of the loading dock in the Loch, and back toward the sea. At the first wide area in the channel the tug "end-for-ended" the Liberty and "turned her loose".

With the tug trailing astern, the Harbor and Channel Pilots easily conned the ship clear of land and when the Pearl Harbor Sea Buoy was abeam, the tug came alongside to starboard and gathered these uniformed Navy men, turned back and made for the Harbor entrance. When the pilots departed, the liberty swung to a Westerly heading. On this occasion, Joey was thinking; "Well, next stop…Pusan."

In retrospect, Joey had been on his Maneuvering Watch Station and observed the entire departure with interest. He was particularly smitten by the strong floral aroma wafting up around him as they turned past and cleared Hospital Point. The thought of all those nurses and patients killed at that location by the Japanese about a decade earlier, in 1941, in their attack on Pearl, made him wonder if he was "correct" in making love to Tomiko. 'After all she was a "countryman" of those attackers'. He put all thoughts of guilt out of his mind and concluded he really did care deeply for that girl... and the war, itself, was "history".

It still was not dinner time but Joey made his way into the Engine Mess and had an ice-filled glass of green "bug juice" and a cookie. He wondered if he should be taking a quick nap when Slim appeared in the doorway...with a big smile on his face, saying: "As ah tol' ya den, glad y'all made it back las' night in tam fo' Watch. Have fun onna beach?" Joey nodded and after swallowing the last of the cookie asked Slim how his liberty went in Waikiki. "Well...ah didn't get waylaid or whupped-up on, so 'suppose it really were a good liberty. An afore ah fo'get, got me a pack o'butts an' didn't fo'get to come-on back hyere. What y'all thank o'dat?" It was Joey's time to smile and say; "Probably should've worried a bit about you an' your wanderin' tendencies...but, so happens, I didn't even think of you after you left the PCT. I was a mite busy...and didn't think about much more than who I was with. By the way, she took all I had to give...and then some. It was a damn good liberty!" Slim grinned and slid onto a seat and "allowed as how" he would have some "bug juice" and a cookie with Joey.

Small talk seemingly over, Joey asked how the Maneuvering Watch went in the Engine Room. Slim said: "Slick as a whistle. The "plant" on dis ship just purrs on answering bells an' dat's also when she "comes t'life". Chief does a little runnin' about up-front, then settles back an' lets de Second do his job. Y'know? Dis recip dudn't even use all d' lube oil we put into her, so ah thank she'a runnin' all right..., and fo' sho', she's "pretty tight". Hope dis continues 'till we get to Korea. Be a real break not to lose tam (time) an' at d'same tam, hav'ta do some heavy un'erway fixin'." Joey again nodded and then said; "Y'know? I still haven't been down below for the engine "light off". Have to get that done before this trip ends. Right now, that's a gap in my sea-goin' education, and by the way, we can still see Oahu and Kauai. Let's go on deck and do some island-eyeballing so I have more to remember about this trip."

Slim got up from his seat in the mess and accompanied Joey to the aft, starboard life line on the Main Deck. Happily there was a westerly wind coming almost "head-on" so the two seamen were clear of any stack gasses…and it was a beautiful, clear evening. Their view was incredible! Slim thanked Joey for getting him topside as he'd; "…hate to'uv missed dis!"

In silence for a half minute or so, they saw the southwest point (Kaiena Point) of Oahu and the highest points of land on Kauai. Joey thought it was almost a shame to have to leave this "Hawaiian island paradise". His mind then shifted to the remainder of the trip to South Korea. "You know, Slim? We still have some 4,450 (nautical) miles to run to get to where we're supposed to, to dump this cargo. That translates to some 17 days of steaming at 11 knots…and that's a lot of steaming to pull off with the Main Engine staying "problem free". Thinking it'll probably be more like 18 or 19 days if the weather acts up any. Hope our cribbage improves 'cause we got a lot of time to burn just getting there." They stayed topside, drinking in the view and engaging in small talk until dinner time when they eased back into the Mess to eat. They got seated early for the meal and that left them with about five hours for "sack-time" prior to being called for the Mid Watch.

"Called" by Big Tom and munching on a sandwich in the Mess, Joey played out in his mind that on his first "watch round" he'd visit the steering engine and give it a fine "look" with a thorough greasing and lubing. Thinking that that piece of machinery just has to stay healthy, he took it upon himself to personally give it all the tender-loving-care it needed…and then some. Joey thought about the deck machinery similarly. When in port and handling cargo, he was the best oiler "the deckies" had seen for lubing and "working" their machinery to a "fine tune". All that cargo handling deck machinery had now been "put to sleep" for the remainder of the trip to Korea …so the engine room auxiliaries, the steering engine and the "reefer plants" took all the Oilers' "watch-round", and "on-deck" time.

Joey's first watch round took him to the Refrigeration (Reefer) Flats and there he saw frost on both "plant's expansion valves", and that was good. He checked the "remote" temperature gauges for the Chill and Freeze Boxes and was made to feel "easier" concerning the Reefer System as a whole. All machinery-mounted gauges showed key temperatures to be in the "normal operating range" …even here in waters where the "normal temperature" is in the "upper 70's". Joey felt the Junior Third Assistant Engineer, the person most directly involved with the Reefers, did a good job in "setting the entire system up" for the rest of the trip…to Korea.

Stopping to get a drink of cold water from a Scuttle-butt (drinking fountain) in the Mid-ship's House passageway, Joey thought he'd take a closer look at the High Pressure (steam operated) Saltwater Evaporator. He knew that making fresh (potable) water took approximately 1 barrel of fuel for every ton of desalinized water "made" by the evaporator… and that made the fresh water quite expensive,… since the evaporator turned out 30 tons of water per day.

Normally, on a watch round, Joey would check all the "evaporator gauges" for readings in the normal, or "green" areas. Should the Oiler find abnormalities, these would be immediately reported to the Engineer on Watch. On this watch, knowing he was still in semi-tropical waters, he made the adjustments himself that were necessary to get all the gauges centered in the "normal" range. While this was exceptionally good "operational engineering practice" and of a level normally handled by licensed engineers, Joey handled it easily and was proud of himself in so doing. Realistically, he thought; "I really don't forget what I'm taught about the proper care of the installed machinery on this Liberty ship…and that's good!"

On his next Watch Round, Joey checked on the Steering Engine and the Reefer Plants but spent most of his time in the engine room working with the Second on mixing-up and applying the chemicals needed for keeping the boiler feed water in the chemically neutral range. The water samples were taken directly from the boilers by means of "water cock-valve spouts" leading to the lower bank of steam generating tubes in each boiler. The water barely met specifications on acidity but was "OK" in "basic" contaminants. The Second explained that "high acidity" would lead to pitting within the tubes… and a "high basic" content would lead to solid scale deposits on the tube interiors, which in turn, would lead to inefficient heat transfer by the generating tubes, hot spots and ultimately, tube failures. Since the deviations from "normal" were quite minor, the second opted to not apply a chemical correction at this time during the watch, but resolved to take another chemical check prior to being relieved of watch duties and apply the proper "correction" at that time. Joey thoroughly appreciated the Second taking the time to explain all this "new stuff" to him.

Following the Watch Joey and Slim both made it to the Engine Mess at the same time. After they both made simple ham and cheese sandwiches and each had poured a glass of orange bug juice, they sat opposite each other in the "coolness" of the Mess, and physically and obviously, relaxed into their chairs. Joey had carried a clean wiping rag up from the "plant" and with it, mopped the sweat off his brow and arms. Slim was the first to speak and he said; "Y'all know, Joey...Ah thank (think) de Second is takin' y'all unner his wing an' turning yo' inta one hell-of-a engineer. Here ah been on Liberty ships since sum tam in '43 an' no-'un has ever taken me aside to teach me feed water chemistry! Ah was lucky t'get the dope on jest standin' Fireman an' Oiler watches.' Y'all keep-on gettin' these "how to's" fum the Second and y'all 'll be ready t-sit fo' yo' third's license when we pay- off".

Joey listened to Slim with both hands raised, palms out toward Slim and shook his head sideways to convey non-concurrence with what Slim had said. He said; "Wait a minute-'r-two... The Chief makes sure you're called out whenever some corrective action is to be taken with the Main (engine)...and at that time no one even knows I exist. Matter-of-fact, I've been learning Black Gang stuff from you since we started in Beaumont." Both men going silent after this verbal exchange allowed them both to hear and feel the engine's "thumping". Listening to the heavy "whump,whump..." Joey thought aloud; "Never thought much about it before but these "recip' rock crushers" are pretty good machines for moving lots of cargo from "A" to "B". They do suffer from a "slow ship's speed" but the engine, and therefore, *the ship does have great reliability and staying power.* ...'Nough of this Bull Crap! Now I think I'll get some rack-time."

Even here in the "semi-tropics", the quarters Slim and Joey shared was quite cool at night. As when they left the Canal Zone, getting it that way required careful adjustment of the topside ventilator scoops so that they pointed directly into the relative wind blowing down the deck above. Bowing to the heat, both seamen went to bed without T-shirts or pajamas…and both were "out cold" within minutes.

CHAPTER TWELVE

STEAMING FOR "WESTPAC"

This nominal 17+ day leg of the SS MC COWAN's voyage to Korea generally followed the reciprocal of the great circle track the Japanese used to gain position for the 7 December 1941 attack on Pearl Harbor. According to the time of year, super-rough water coupled with typhoon-strength winds in this area of the Pacific could turn a routine voyage into a nightmare for a hapless vessel plying this route. But this was the route (the Liberty took) to get to Korea from Oahu. And this was "that time of year"!

Always concerned about the "weather", Joey had kept up with the daily habit of stopping by the Radio Shack, on the 03 Level of the midships house, for a "weather report" from "Sparks", the ship's radioman, and that weather report also included a "best-rationalized" prediction of upcoming weather. The radios told Sparks that there was a "good sized Low" forming a day ahead on the Liberty's track. On this, the third day of this leg, Sparks wondered aloud to Joey; whether or not the Skipper would alter course southward to skirt this "problem weather". Joey just shrugged his shoulders allowing as how he really didn't know what the Skipper would decide.

"Bad weather predictions", per se, meant to the entire ship's company that steps should be taken to "batten down the hatches", thereby securing the ship against some weather-caused disabling accidents. The first area that entered Joey's mind as needing some corrective action, was the

61

Machine Shop and its overloaded round stock and pipe metal stowage racks and spaces. Joey went to the machine shop to talk directly to the Machinist (Mac) and impart to that man, his "take" on the upcoming weather.

Mac's first reaction was to spit out the word; "Shit!" Then sizing Joey up for the increased level of physical activity required to square-away his spaces, the Machinist asked Joey if he was available to help with this chore; "...now!" Joey said; "Sure, just as long as it doesn't extend beyond supper...and my needed rest period before the Midwatch. Now ...give me a minute or two to scare-up some help." With that comment, Joey headed out of the shop, and continued up toward the engineering berthing area...and Slim.

Upon his arrival at his berthing space he noted that Slim had already lashed down the desk and chair...and his and Joey's lockers. Impressed, Joey asked how he, Slim, had gotten the word about the coming stormy weather. Slim responded that the Chief had called the Engine Room and passed the word along...and directed that the watch start battening down every normally loose item in the "Plant", and that's what the 4-8 Watch is doing now,...finishing the *lash-down*".

It was almost imperceptible but Joey felt the bow of the ship dip below the horizontal and take on a large swell. The shudder that ran through the ship removed all doubt about whether or not the storm "had begun". The ship remained somewhat stable beam to beam but the "pitching" was increasing in severity. Joey said; "It's on us! I was just with Mac and he needs some help...right now. That shop is a disaster ready to happen. I'm going back down there. Think, with your help, we can get the lashings in place prior to supper." Slim just shrugged and said; "What're we waiting fo'? Let's he'p Mac... might really need his talents sooner dan we 'spect."

With that, both seamen trotted out of the space and went directly to the Machine Shop. Mac was found bracing himself against the ship's motion and trying to make a neat bundle out of a mess of brass piping (loaded on the ship to replace, as needed, damaged sea-water piping). He wasn't very successful in doing that. Joey relieved Mac of the 21-thread Manila line he was using for the lash down and Slim gathered up a second and final load of brass pipes. Joey tied both bundles up neatly and they were deposited back on their individual stowage rack…, in order to be lashed to those racks…, which Joey did next. The trio went next to the solid, bar or round metal solid stock, which, like the pipes, were nowhere where they had to be for proper storm stowage. In the main, this stock was quite heavy by the piece, and so had to be separately handled…, again, by the piece.

Joey and Slim did this latter portion of the "storm prep's" while Mac looked to securing the large "machine" tools. Joey watch closely as Mac used clamps to fix the traveling stock-holder tray on the Southbend Lathe, took the mounting adjustments "to the stops" on the shop shaper, on the 8 inch grinder, the drill press, and then placed in lockers, the portable electric drills and other hand tools. Joey was impressed with Mac's knowledge of his machine tools, and thought he handled their "securing", perfectly! He also thought that all loose items such as trays of machined tool bits, chucks, spare grinder wheels, hand tools and machine-tool holders were also correctly deposited in lockers, and the Oxygen and other gas bottles were properly lashed to the "lightening holes" in the ship's beaming.

Finally, other than needing a sweep-down to clean the deck of metal cuttings, the shop was declared "storm ready" by Slim. Mac just nodded…and it was dinner time, so Mac was left alone in his shop.

On their way to the Mess, Joey mumbled to Slim that he hoped the guys on watch took care of the "securing needs" in the Engine Room…as he had done enough "securing" in the Machine Shop. Slim just nodded.

Since it was still relatively early in the "storm game", supper was able to be cooked, hence "served hot". Almost like a "last meal for the condemned", this meal was of the "holiday variety". It consisted of roast beef, thickened gravy, mashed spuds, beans and warm rolls. There were also nicely prepared bowls of fresh veggie salad on the mess tables.

It should be noted that the best possible preparations for the storm by the cooks and mess men were taken so that the food on the tables didn't slide off them because of heavy ship motion in the storm. This was actually accomplished through the usage of damp toweling to cover the tables. This simple ploy made the serving of freshly cooked food a possibility…because the dishes in use for the meal were heavy enough to stick to the toweling that, in turn, stuck to the tables. Utensils were wrapped in damp, but very clean, toweling as well. Because of this prior preparation of the tables, Joey thanked the Messman in the Engine Mess. Of note, the Messman was a young, lanky and almost always smiling Negro named Otis. Otis, still smiling, "made believe" in tipping his (nonexistent) cap at Joey's compliment.

Keeping drink materials on the tables was another story entirely. Glasses were filled by the Mess man on a "as needed basis". His pitchers of drink were stowed on a shelf in the "center (between tables) island"… as were the bottles and jars of spices. Glasses and cups were issued to the diners as requested and then became the responsibility of the user to keep them from falling and breaking. Many a glass was stowed between the knees, between sips.

The meal was a winner! Joey and Slim left the Mess fully satiated. They went to a lee space just aft of the center house to enjoy an outdoor smoke before heading for their beds and as much rest as possible… in the time remaining before being hit with the even higher, building storm seas that would soon toss them around with an even greater vengeance. They noted distinct and heavy swells hitting the ship from almost dead ahead. The ship was pitching and they thought the main deck was almost awash with the crests of these swells as they "passed aft". The winds buffeting the ship were more than moderate and were hitting the ship broad on the port bow.

Joey knew the sea and wind severity would increase as the storm enveloped the ship. Nudging his watch mate, he shouted; "Hey Slim; learned at the Sheepshead Bay school how to find the storm center…and from that, determine, up to a point… whether or not the ship's course is optimal for missing the highest levels of storm fury. Here… I'll, show you." With that, Joey led Slim forward of the house, and took position on the ship's centerline. He said; "First, face directly into the true wind. When we're in the Northern Hemisphere, so raise your right arm straight to the right and keep it stiff. Your arm will point to the storm's center. Now, how you use the information you just got is important!

In these waters, in this hemisphere, the story gets important to get it right! Smart money says that to get away from the storm, put the storm center on the starboard quarter and steam out of the whole mess. If the game of probability of storm movement is followed by Mother Nature, the storm itself will help you get clear by pushing you with mostly a quartering wind toward calmer water… and away from the center. All that crap says; if this is a biggie of a storm, then we should already be altering course to the Southwest for optimum storm evasion."

Slim had paid close attention to Joey's monologue and shrugged while saying; "Sounds lak a real good plan but lak wif most plans, s'pose Mom Nature doan cooperate and the storm changes course on ya'…an' dat plan goes down de shitter. What you gonna do den?"

"Same as what you did the first time… Get a new fix on storm center and maneuver as before, to clear it all. That bad and unpredictable stuff happens…and often, too!"

CHAPTER THIRTEEN

AND IT WENT; BUMP

It should be noted that the ship did not alter its course during the next several minutes that Joey and Slim were on deck. The seas were building and the wind was increasing and a trip to see Sparks let Joey know that the storm, coming up from the South and strengthening, was due to increase in severity as it hit the Latitude of the Japanese islands, (a fact already suspected by Joey)... and then would head in a slight East by Northeasterly direction.

In a way that was good news for the MC GOWAN. With a modest course correction to the Southwest the ship would be heading into the weaker storm quadrant and the majority of the storm affected sea- area would continue to pass quickly to the North of the Liberty ship. Sparks received an updated SITREP (Situation Report) from the Skipper to send to the ship's operator, American President Lines (APL). The Report was, in reality, a weather and "impact to progress on the track" report and did note that due to storm impact to the ship's track, the ship already lost approximately two hours (22 Nautical Miles) of the planned track "Speed Of Advance" (SOA). At the time the message was sent, that amounted to a full 2 hours that had to be added to the Estimated Time of Arrival (ETA) in Pusan. Joey thought this was the ending of weather-caused delays to be expected as the ship transited North in Latitude while conforming to the Great Circle route to Pusan.

Before the Liberty clears it, this storm alone should delay arrival (ETA) by 3-5 hours.

"Sleep" was out of the question for Joey and Slim and Joey felt that most of the crew was similarly affected. Joey was well past the "getting seasick" portion of going to sea to make a living. It was just that the pounding resulting from the ship heading into the sea kept them close to be unceremoniously dumped from their beds…with the next large swell. They spent too much time just trying to keep from falling to the deck! Joey was the first to offer verbal complaints about their unsatisfactory situation and he concluded these with; "Going into the Mess Decks and maybe help the cook or mess man with getting breakfast ready. Maybe some coffee will finish getting me awake and help get me back to some sense of reality.

With a hot grill, the cook would do fine with fried eggs, bacon and ham but would have problems keeping the stir-pots of pancake, waffle mix and hot cereal under control. Joey did help the mess man with getting the damp toweling in place on the tables and with making perked coffee and filling the pitchers with orange fruit juices. Joey knew the mess man's first name was Otis…but for some unknown reason, had never used the name in conversation with the man. This day was different and storm not-withstanding, Joey felt like talking…so Otis heard his name often this morning.

Normally very quiet and sensitive to the racial biases of the Texans and other southerners in the "Black Gang", Otis became quite outgoing and loquacious with Joey. He seemed to take on a new life when Joey told him that he had "mess-cooked" on his first trip at sea, on a T-2 tanker. "Hey Otis…" Joey said. "Where're you from? Come aboard like most of the rest of us, in Beaumont?"

Otis came back with; "Yep! Was playing some semi-pro baseball in a Negro League in East Texas when I was recruited for this ship by a Marine Cooks and Stewards Union dude. The man promised lots of OT (over-time) bucks from this APL-flagged ship, kinda' like what happens on the West Coast where APL operates out of. So far nothing out of the "usual" has happened here…an' I ain't getting' rich on this ship. On the "good" side, working for this (Engine Mess) cook and waiting on this bunch of engineering types like y'all, has combined to be a winner. I like this job!"

By this point in the conversation the Black Gang started arriving for breakfast..., and the discourse between Joey and Otis ended. Slim was the first to take his seat at the table and Joey beat Otis in explaining to Slim that pancakes were not on the menu because of the heavy seas... but that just about everything else on the regular menu, was. With a smile, Slim sarcastically came back with; "You doin' the servin', Joey?" Then, with Joey's shaking of his head "No!", Slim asked Otis to just bring him his "regular" breakfast fare. Slim then patted the seat next to his and gestured for Joey to join him for breakfast. Joey readily took the seat and told Otis; "Ditto. Just bring me my regular breakfast, too."

While the cook had been mentally debating whether or not to scratch off the menu some of the key breakfast items such as fried eggs due to the heavy ship motion in the storm, he neglected to make that hard decision prior to Slim ordering his meal. The Cook hid his reluctance to handle "runny" items and actually filled Slim's order. Joey was pleased with the cook's decision. Joey's final thought prior to breakfast was; "To hell with the storm! I'm hungry and I'm going to eat!"

Wrestling with keeping the liquids in their containers and off the deck, and just hanging-on to one's spot at the table made sitting at the tables a chore. For a while it appeared the storm was going to be the victor in this battle...but the seamen were resolute in getting and eating their breakfasts; hence, were the real winners. No one got seasick and only a crumb or two made it down to the deck.

Breakfast came and went and Joey had until 11:30 before he'd be "called for" the noon watch. He decided that after his post-meal smoke, he'd head into the engine room and get with Big Tom for pointers on the "engine light-off" procedure...even if the engine was running. He caught Tom between rounds and in a receptive mode to act as a teacher for a while. They talked about the weather and high seas for a few minutes...deciding that the weather was already abating and probably by the time Joey took the watch; "...things'd be back to normal."

According to Tom, the "biggee" with lighting off this main engine was insuring all three "Units" making up the engine were "separately and properly warmed up". Also, since the engine and propeller shaft were coupled together, the shaft had to be locked by using the "jacking gear" to keep it from rotating…and maybe putting the propeller in danger of fouling or something. With those thoughts in mind, the steam to be used to warm the engine, could, over a normally two hour period, be slowly and carefully "cut in" to the three engine unit jackets, cylinders and finally, unit drains. This steam was obtained using the Main Engine Throttle Valve System… and the resulting exhaust steam and condensate would be "drained" to the bilges until the condenser was operational and became the "draining point". A small loss of Feed Water was to be expected. For "light-off", as when operating normally, the steam went to the cylinders in sequence (High Pressure, Intermediate Pressure and Low Pressure) with bypass valves in each unit cracked open. While Joey really had this information down pat, he still needed to actually be part of the team that made it all happen. "Nothing like a little practical experience…" he thought. Prior to leaving the engine spaces, Joey thanked Big Tom for taking the time to "educate" him.

The weather was definitely improving and Joey found he was no longer "hanging on to stuff" to keep upright. He made it back to his berthing area and noted that Slim was sound asleep. His admiration for Slim and his ability to catch some sleep in the worst of situations forced Joey to smile. He really liked his watch mate and was looking forward to "hitting the beach" with him when they got to Pusan. Joey didn't know of any Waikiki-like areas of Pusan that Slim's wife might sic him on to; so he should be available for some fun in Pusan. Joey thought.

There was still a few hours remaining before Joey was to be called for his watch, so he chose to climb up to his bunk and get some sleep… if possible. As Joey suspected, the Low Pressure "weather bubble" that had rocked the ship, was a very fast moving system that was quickly passing to the North of the Liberty; so now the ocean in the immediate vicinity was definitely becoming calmer. Joey went to sleep.

For the next week and a half the ship plied the great circle route to a point in the Sea of Japan, South of but close aboard the major Japanese

Island of Honshu. The weather encountered on this route was anything but pleasant. Minor weather disturbances dogged the ship and kept the ship, with short exceptions, in what seemed to be constant rain. For the oilers, the watch rounds that took them on deck, were done in "the cold". Oilers kept water proof jackets stowed high (in the engine room fidley) near the boiler air-feed Economizers, where they would be kept warm and dry until the "next topside round" was to be taken. Seamen, being no different than most folks working and living ashore, were subject to getting the weather-induced, extended "grays", which resulted in their being somewhat depressed. Along with the overall, and extended, bad weather, such was the case on the MC GOWAN.

With "depressed seamen" or not, the ship continued on its passage to Japan (then to Korea). The generally bad weather blowing in, bow on, had its adverse affect on the SOA the ship was capable of making. The projected Position of Intended Movement (PIM) requiring eleven knots for ship speed had not been possible since the day the small storm blew on them. The newest track data radioed to APL showed the ship (making ten vs. the planned eleven knots) arriving in Pusan almost two days later than previously thought;…and the generally crappy weather did not abate until the Liberty sailed into the North-flowing but warm, Japanese Current.

While the skies were still cloudy and overcast, the temperature started a climb a day prior to the ship's arrival in Japan's Inland Sea. The Oilers noted they no longer needed jackets for the topside portion of their watch-rounds. The warmer air was definitely welcome.

From the western edge of the Japanese Current to when the ship would start the final 100 nm of the transit to Pusan, there was still some 250 nm (one day's transit at 11 knots) of transit left to go in the Inland Sea. While "Safe Waters" for transit were well marked on the chart in use, since the Liberty was not RADAR equipped, *good visibility was still an absolute necessity for a safe transit*. The ship entered the Inland Sea at dusk and the sky was overcast.

Early in the transit West through the Japanese islands, a Low Pressure front passed over the southerly islands of Shikoku and Kyushu. This Low brought even poorer visibility with it. Still, the ship actually cleared the southern coast of the main island of Honshu, visually using the navigation aids (NavAids) on that island with little trouble.

Clearing the northern coast of Kyushu prior to departing the Inland Sea was another story. When the Liberty was on this portion of the track, it was night-time and pitch black, and heavily overcast. Physically, the MC GOWAN was off the northern tip of Kyushu during this period of low visibility. NavAids were not visible! This lack of good visibility caused the ship to close the landmass, and unknowingly wound up in the red-charted "Navigation Dangerous Zone" in clearing Kyushu. And, *she did not clear the rocky northwestern Kyushu tip* in "safe waters".

Joey had just gone to his bunk following the evening meal and had swung himself up onto his mattress when the ship first bounced off the rocks. He was in the air and heading for the deck when the ship bounced again and leaned heavily to starboard. Gripping one of the rails of his bunk kept Joey from having a serious collision with the deck. Never-the-less, he still hit it hard, even if on his feet when doing so. In the lower bunk, slim merely bounced high and into the bottom of Joey's bunk. He yelled to Joey; "What in hell jest happened?" Joey wasn't talking as he was just trying to keep from getting some broken bones while bouncing. Slim continued with; "Thank we run this hummer aground?" Joey answered this query with; "Think that's what happened... and that's for sure! What else'd have us upside down and bouncing? Think we'd better get on down to the Plant...they're sure to have taken some damage down there." With that both Joey and Slim pulled on their shoes and "bolted" through the joiner door and down to the Engine Room.

CHAPTER FOURTEEN

WE'RE THERE; PUSAN

The grounding was hard on the MC GOWAN. As was thought by all aboard, "the bouncing" was certain to have resulted in monstrous stresses and bends to the ship's keel and bottom, and also to the structural "beam to beam" strength members. In Joey's engineering thoughts; "...who knows the extent of the peripheral misalignments to our machinery foundations that were also suffered." The fact that Joey and Slim immediately headed to the engine room to make themselves available for the upcoming damage control effort spoke volumes about their dedication to the welfare of the entire ship and its people. *Down into the Engine Room they ran!*

When they arrived in the plant, the engine room watch was checking "all the corners and piping systems" in the space for leaks. The Chief Engineer was right behind Joey and Slim, and had "zipped down" the ladders as well. Joey reported to the watch engineer (the First Assistant Engineer) and asked him how he, Joey, could be of help. The First didn't hesitate a moment in telling Joey to get "Fuel Oil Tank "soundings" (measurements on the volume of fuel oil remaining in the ship's double-bottom storage tanks). Slim was sent to check-on and report findings of flooding in the bilges in the engine room, shaft Alley, and in the Refrigeration Spaces and Cargo Holds. Big Tom made it down to the engine room at about this time and was next in line, after Slim, to get instructions on how he could help. Joey was long gone by the time Tom and his Fireman got their instructions.

Joey wasted no time in doing this Fuel Oil storage check and jotting his findings down on a small pad of paper. When finished he took his findings back to the First Assistant who was then talking to the Chief. In addition to the written findings, Joey let the Engineers know that *sea water was coming out of all the bottom FO tank pet-cocks*. The Chief then stated the obvious; "It's a wonder we're still afloat, but… we got some fuel left in the two Settling Tanks on service here down in the engine room and, with care, that should be enough to get us to Pusan! Gotta let the Skipper know this generally crappy news and also, that our draft has been increased because of the tank flooding. Think, to make it to Pusan without a tow, we're gonna have to "save steam" an' that means; kill the evap's (fresh water makers) and some of the other "nice to have", steam operated machinery. Don't think we'll have to kill one of the boilers, though…we're not that short of fuel. In a way, I'm happy we're as close to mooring at a well-equipped pier as we will be in Pusan. Be big-time embarrassing if'n we're towed into port like a dead-stick-water-barge!"

With that pronouncement the chief eased over to the sound-powered telephone. Rang up the bridge and said; "Hi Captain. (The greeting was done with a "smiley face".) Here's the "lower level news: On the good side of the ledger; we can make it to Pusan, and to a fuel barge there, with what we've got left, if we don't waste any. Bad news is; we're deeper in the water an', for sure, it's gonna take an extended tour in a dry-dock to repair this ship. Think most of the (flat) bottom plating took some real damage. There's nothing but sea water coming through the (bottom) FO Stowage Tank Sounding Petcocks. Have a man checking the Steering Engine…but think it's OK. Don't know how, but the shaft still appears true and we're not getting the screw vibrations I'd expect after the ship hit the bottom like it did. Probably missed the rudder and prop entirely. Judging from the extent of the damage, there'll be some drag…but think we can give you (the standard) turns for 11 knots all the way in…weather permitting. We'll be double checking for hot-running bearings."

Hearing the Skipper's response, the Chief came back with; "Just ring us up the bell...for the record; and we're back to 76 turns." And he hung up the phone. To the listening-in "black gang" members in attendance, the Chief confided; "Don't know what the speed over the ground will be then but standard turns for a "Full bell" will be the most that we will coax from this power plant..." Then, after a grimace, added; " if, with the damage to the bottom, we can reach and keep that number of turns."

The First Assistant heard it all and let the chief know; "I'll make all that happen!" and he turned to speak with the Fireman-Water Tender. Joey then departed the engine room to satisfy himself as to it's "running health", and then eased down into the Steering Engine Room to check the entire steering system. All was well. Joey then left the stern for the Engine Mess... with a smile.

Back in the Mess, Joey and Slim took seats with the 8 to 12 Watch guys, Big Tom and his Fireman, Stan Erlichman. Stan was a New Yorker and like Joey, was new to Liberty ships... and this was his first trip on one. Stan and Joey looked to the "WW II veterans", Big Tom and Slim, for "expert opinions and facts" regarding the "MC GOWAN breed of ship". Joey opened the discussion with: "Hey you two veterans! Been through one of these "bottom thumpers" before...or been around for the "fix-it time" in a shipyard? We gonna stick with the ship in a yard or be sent home? Any guesses?"

Both Tom and Slim glanced at each other, then Tom responded with; "No...on the groundings but was on board one that got torpedoed in WW II. We stayed afloat but had bad flooding from the damage the "fish" caused. We, the crew, were kept on board to get the ship into a yard and into dry dock...but after that we were shipped back to the port where we'd signed onto that ship. Guess, in those days, we were most needed to crew up the "new construction" Liberty ships as soon as they slid down the ways. Different set of circumstances back then." Tom then said; "Do you remember the WW II poster ad that had a sinking ship and this dude with a sea bag saying; "Damn right I'm going back to sea!... or something like that?" Both Joey and Stan just nodded. They recalled the poster ad but were too young to have started shipping-out at the time, so, both had ignored the poster's "call".

Tom continued talking with; "Anyway; never mind that. All that said, I do think we'll be going into dry dock somewhere near to here; and as soon as it can happen after our cargo has been unloaded. And yes, I think we'll be staying with the ship until it's fixed and goes home to the States. You know? I really don't know what they'll be having us do to earn our paychecks while we're in dock." Joey nodded his understanding and echoing the Chief Engineer, mumbled; "Sure hope we don't wind up getting towed to the fix-it yard. That'd be embarrassing as hell!"

The ship actually crept north to Pusan at an SOA of about 8 knots for the remaining few miles. The foul weather had passed, and other than the chill in the air, it was like what it was, an "early spring" day. Joey was aft in an "observation mode" when they passed through the huge entrance of Pusan harbor. A tug met them as they cleared the seawall, and then made up to the Liberty with two "breast lines". This was recommended for fore and aft pushing by the tug. The tug then finished its tie-up with a neatly appearing "alongside to starboard attitude".

They arrived at the harbor entrance during Joey's 12 to 4 PM Watch. Joey had been topside for the Maneuvering Watch (called prior to the tug tie-up) and attentively watched as the ship passed close aboard to the anchorages of five hospital ships in the harbor. These WW II ships had been activated from the US Navy's Reserve Fleet for the Korean War. Joey had read in the newspaper that the Pacific Fleet Reserve anchorage used (between the wars) was north of San Francisco and in the Bay; so concluded, that was where they were stowed. Further, these hospital ships were well-laid-up, so that there was minimum effort needed to get them back to sea.

On this day, around each of them was a "bee hive" of activity as their small boats and helicopters were plying the sea lanes in the harbor between the mooring pier and the hospital ships' "small craft landing areas". Joey later found out that these small craft and the attending "helos" were carrying the wounded and dead to those hospital ships from trains that had come in from the battle perimeter ringing Pusan to the North. Within minutes Joey saw that the train-yard tracks and discharge areas were close aboard and parallel to the cargo-landing docks that the SS MC GOWAN would use to discharge cargo. Looking beyond the mooring area he also saw that when moored, the Liberty ship would be close to the security gate leading to an "older, downtown section" of the city of Pusan.

CHAPTER FIFTEEN

ALONGSIDE IN PUSAN

After his watch was relieved at 4 PM, Joey dropped down to the engine room to look up the Second Assistant to get his "OK" to go on liberty after the mooring was completed... and liberty, per se, was further "OK'd" by the Skipper. (The Second's "OK" was dependent upon whether or not finishing "unfinished" ship's work would take priority over the crew going on liberty). The "unfinished work" was still going on.

Tying up the MC GOWAM was routinely accomplished ...even with her bottom "tore-up" from the grounding. Joey stayed on deck following the securing of the Maneuvering Watch. He knew he'd be needed when the ship would be taking on fuel... and that was certain to happen "soon". He also knew that the Skipper would also quickly replenish the currently depleted food stocks and other consumables. Joey (correctly) assumed that the both the Deck and Engine Watches would formally be kept on deck to augment the cooks and stewards in handling the "food stores" that would also be arriving "as soon as possible".

First to arrive was the self-propelled Fuel Oil (FO) Barge. The barge lines were taken aboard by Joey and an AB and the barge then was tied up alongside to starboard. The "FO" hoses were taken aboard by Joey and Big Tom...but there were no undamaged piping and stowage tanks to hook them up to. All the lower connected piping leading from the FO Manifold to the ship's FO stowage tanks, and the tanks themselves, had been torn by the grounding. So, to augment the ship's relatively small FO Service Tanks located below decks in the Engine Room, the only on board FO stowage, Big Tom got together with the Koreans manning the barge and inquired as to whether some "good-sized, portable FO tanks" could be obtained and placed on the Liberty's main deck close to the manifold. The Koreans understood Tom, nodded and immediately departed to arrange for delivery of these portable tanks.

While the engineering watch members were "handling" the FO Barge, the remainder of the consumable-replacement cargo was being delivered to the ship by means of "2 ½ Ton" trucks and shore-based cranes riding the railroad tracks on the mooring pier the ship was were tied up to. Korean laborers boarded the Liberty to stow these consumables in their proper, below decks, shipboard holds and other designated spaces. During the relatively short delay-related intervals experienced in the consumable stores load-out, the ship off-loaded her deck cargo of trucks, weapons and ammunition. Joey was impressed by how seamlessly and safely these overlapping operations were carried out. When not busy with hooking-up shore- based "house- keeping services" to the ship, Joey closely watched the "fresh and frozen" food-stuffs being loaded aboard, and with a smile, thought; "We're gonna eat real good! …Yeah!"

Also during that first evening alongside in Pusan, in addition to participating in the off-loading of MC GOWAN's deck cargo and the taking aboard of fuel and consumables, the crew was also invited to the Skipper's office to make "a money-draw" against their earned wages up to this point in the trip. "US Military Script" (money) was used to pay the seamen, to finance their "liberty expenditures" ashore in Pusan.

It was explained to the seamen that use of regular US money/ currency was seriously discouraged and that money, already possessed by crew members, was to be left aboard the ship (and the Skipper volunteered use of the ship's safe for this purpose.) The rationale for this precautionary shift in monies was explained as follows; "Having the US currency in circulation in Korea would contribute to the (Korean) counterfeiting of US bills". Joey found it hard to believe that negating counterfeiting was the real reason for using script, but that was what was "advertised". "So be it." Joey thought. "As long as this stuff spends, all is well with me!"

Joey dropped down to his quarters and shifted attire into clothing fit for liberty and the "much cooler temperatures" arriving with the Northerly wind and the setting sun. The weather, from late evening through the night, was predicted to be "picture-perfectly" clear and windy, with the wind continuing to blow in from the North-Northwestern quadrant of Asia...; from Siberia. To expect "cooler temperatures" of the air coming in from Siberia was euphemistic, since, at this time of year, that "air" got downright cold with the oncoming dusk! Asking one of the Korean stevedores what the Korean word for "cold" was, he was told with a graphic "shiver" by the Korean that it was "*chupta*". Joey would not forget that word!

Joey did not eat his dinner on board. He knew he was going to be ashore at least five hours before he had to take the Midnight to Four Watch and felt that the five hours was more than enough time on liberty, to work in something new to him...a Korean meal. Upon treading down the companionway from the ship, Joey saw the Pusan Harbor Main Gate forward of the ship. It was close; only about 100 yards ahead. This gate was in the immediate vicinity of the entering trains' railroad track turning area,... where the trains would use either the tracks heading down the docks or those a bit inland of the docks to where the waterfront warehouses stood. At the corner of the security fence and the pier-side road there was the Military Police guard shack servicing the Gate. Joey was holding his seaman's papers (a plastic coated card with his photo on it) for the MPs to check when one of them volunteered the advice that Joey should watch his step when in-town, since; "...earlier today, a fellow was killed outside the Seamen's Club.

Seems like a shoeshine kid was working on the seaman's boots and the seaman was stoned-drunk. The kid pulled the pin on a grenade he had in his box and took off running. The seaman didn't know what was happening and the box exploded taking that seaman's leg with it. He died right there, on the sidewalk. Joey thanked the MP for the "heads-up", and confirmed that to get to town one had to use one of the busses in the Park. He then turned for the open gate where the road led to the Bus Parking Area. In this Bus Park there were several busses of the widely utilized, yellow, "school bus" type, commonly seen in the US.

In addition to Joey and a couple of the Liberty ship's deck seamen walking toward these busses, there were also many arriving Korean dock workers that had finished their afternoon shift and were (probably) heading home. Joey immediately rationalized that with adding the off-going pier workers, there could generally, be a seating problem on the busses, so he hurried toward the busses at a jog to claim a seat. He was successful.

This was the "New Yorker" in Joey showing itself. Why? He really didn't know how far into Pusan he'd be traveling, so really, not having a seat would be just fine if the trip was in the "short range" category. While Joey didn't take the chance on possibly standing for a prolonged period, he grabbed a seat…simply because it was available.

The busses had their destinations noted in signs above the driver's front window. Joey selected one that serviced the "Youngdo Gu Beach Area" and "Downtown Pusan". Climbing aboard Joey asked the driver; "What's the schedule this bus will follow?" The driver stared at Joey dumbly…not understanding the question. One of the Koreans boarding at the time understood Joey and took it upon himself to respond to the question. In perfect English he told Joey; "This bus will make all of its stops to the beach within a half hour of leaving here. It will wait at the beach-end of the run for ten minutes and then return… making the same stops." Joey thanked the translator and then asked; "Any good local restaurants on the run that you'd recommend?" The Korean said; "Yes. Get off at the Main Railroad Station stop in the old city, in the Haeundai District, and go to the Pusan Hotel right across the street from the station. The restaurant there serves the best food currently commercially available in Pusan…, what with the war going on and all."

Joey was surprised by this Korean's capability to speak the English language perfectly… and in his grasp of Joey's desires in finding good food. Joey thanked the man and reached out to shake his hand. The now smiling Korean took Joey's hand and shook it warmly…and Joey then said; "Now if you'll just take a moment more and let the driver know where to drop me off, I'll not bother you anymore." The Korean nodded and did as Joey asked. The driver was nodding his understanding when the bus left the waterfront's Main Gate area.

CHAPTER SIXTEEN

———— ✥ ————

WHERE THE ACTION IS

Following the main route out of the gate area the bus passed close aboard a small, stucco and wooden plank sided, Catholic Church; …cross on the steeple and all. From the American's perspective, the church was tiny and currently unoccupied, and had Joey impressed that it was: there in Korea at all, and representing Christianity. Then, putting the waterfront behind them, the bus swung directly away from the harbor and toward the downtown area. Joey noted that other than a few jeeps and military 2 & 1/2 ton trucks, the streets were mostly empty. There was virtually no one just strolling about. He also saw that the buildings on either side of the road were mostly one and two-story, "seedy" residences that looked as if they had spent the last twenty five years at least, in a dilapidated status. Joey thought; "It was certain that with the current state of maintenance of these private homes and the "official" city's structures, the recently departed "occupying Japanese" had not been kind to Korea."

Not depending on the man's memory, when the bus reached the city square that housed the Main Train Station, Joey reached over from his front row seat and touched the driver's arm. The hand-signal to stop the bus was given by Joey and the driver complied. Joey stood to depart and asked his translator if he could later pick-up the bus from the same place he was being let off. The "translator" determined that Joey could do that and passed that information along to him. While it was getting late and past "evening star time", there still was a tiny bit of daylight illuminating the western sky and in that fading daylight, Joey saw well the immediate neighborhood. He noted that the Train Station neighborhood, while not "deserted", was very lightly populated ...with folks looking like they were in a hurry to get home. Joey wondered "...why the rush?" and came to the conclusion that it was probably the result of the nation being at war with the "North",...whose people looked and thought like those here, below the 38th Parallel, in the South. He rationalized that these people in Pusan knew they probably had infiltrating Northerners amongst them and that thought might have frightened them...hence the "hustle home".

Joey had stepped off the bus diagonally across the road from the Pusan Hotel... and its, by reputation; "...the best food in town" restaurant. He did not waste any time in going into the restaurant and making himself comfortable. The "waitress" turned out to be middle-aged, wearing clean western serving attire and was actually one of the place's owners. She knew her restaurant's offered fare quite well and by memory, recited the menu for Joey. Her English speaking abilities however, were limited, but Joey understood her.

The food she recommended was modeled in Plaster of Paris and was lacquer painted and displayed in a glass enclosed turn table just inside the restaurant entry door. The plated, painted models looked as the food would look when presented at the table. An entering customer could not miss seeing all these foods and would use the establishment's menu mainly to determine item prices and written or verbal descriptions of the food. The menu was written in Korean pictographic characters and also in English. The waitress pointed to her dinner recommendation in the menu. It was a small poached fish and some cooked vegetables. The dish came with a side portion of Kimchee, which was a native Korean, pickled, garlic laden, fish-sauce served over over thinly sliced cabbage leaves. Kimchee was heavily used in Korea to add to the flavor of most of the main menu items, and also to add a most awful stink of garlic on the diner's breath. With a smile and remembering the Second Assistant' comment at the Pearl City Tavern, Joey thought of this evening's future romantic ventures being adversely impacted by his dinner. Since he was prepared to pay for his expected female companion later this evening, he cared little about his breath.

He washed his dinner down with a beer, as the MPs at the Gate mentioned that in most areas of Pusan, the purity and taste of the town water was questionable. In some areas of thought, Joey was not a gambler. "What he ate and drank" was such an area. Strolling from the restaurant, Joey had left his jacket open. After a few steps however, he felt the bight of the cold "Siberian winds" blowing against him and quickly buttoned up the garment. His wait for the bus on its trip to the beach area was thankfully only a couple of minutes.

While the bus ride was free, he still carried his "Seaman's Papers" card in his hand and was prepared to show it if so asked by the driver or other "authority". The driver did not ask to see Joey's identification. Rumbling toward the western Pusan beach area, Joey stayed cold; riding in a bus or not. He didn't shiver…but he was cold!

Unlike the bus he was on earlier, this bus was crowded with 40 or more riders. While not seated, Joey made use of the opportunity to carry on a conversation with fellow, English speaking, passengers. The ride to the beach area took some ten minutes from the train station. Joey used that time to ascertain that the western stretch of Pusan's beach area had morphed into somewhat of a strip-mall. He was to find that the "mall" offered a visiting seaman everything from bar seating, through booze and prostitution, and included one or two good restaurants, and several good retail sales stores. He decided, cold weather or not, to take his time while "shopping" the mall.

The bus stopped and disgorged its load of the forty-odd American seamen and Korean harbor workers. To a man they started walking-up the mall. Most stopped at the first, and northern-most restaurant whose sign was professionally printed in English and read: "Kim's Restaurant" on the top line, "Burgers and Hot Dogs" on the second line and "Script Accepted" on the third line. Joey felt better knowing that the military script that was issued to him instead of "American greenbacks" was "the coin of the realm".

He also noted there appeared to be an inordinate number of young, draft- age male Koreans …just "hanging around" the mall. By a lopsided majority, these Korean young men wore, what appeared to be, cast- off American jeans or US Army fatigue trousers, paratrooper boots, and leather flight jackets or US Navy issued pea coats. How they came by these items would remain a mystery to Joey. Joey also noted a scarcity of youngish, under the age of fifty, women or girls. To this point, Joey saw none.

Not missing much that the beginning of the mall had to offer and the places of business that were doing the "offering", Joey came to the conclusion that Coney Island, in Brooklyn, had nothing to worry about. It had little to fear from the competition of the "seedy" Pusan Western Beach Mall. Huddled against the cold wind, Joey came upon a candy vendor that was working the area nearer to the bus stop, and purchased from the man a sesame seed and honey", candy bar" that he thought; "… is to also be my desert tonight." The bar was quite chewy but tasted fine!

Opting to get out of the wind, Joey entered a "Photo Studio"-named, pitched tent that advertised; "Send a Photo Home" on a hand painted sign on canvas cloth mounted on the tent. The sign had flapped noisily in the wind and was therefore an attention-getter. Joey thought, as the sign suggested, he should get a photo of himself to send to his mother. Entering the tent he checked out his appearance in a readily available mirror, that was hung onto one of the tent's main supports, precisely for this purpose. He saw a scraggly-bearded, unkempt and somewhat tired looking youngster looking back at him. The photographer was not fluent in English but carried the message for where he wanted Joey to sit and when to smile. His equipment actually looked like it was last used during the American Civil War.

The photographer held up a pan of flash powder, and ducking under an attached-to-the-camera, canvas cloth, raised the pan…; said "smile" in English and fired off the powder. The resulting "tin-type" looking photo was as Joey expected …not very flattering. He looked like what he was; a twenty-plus year old whose beard was unkempt and a bit thin and who had dark circles under his eyes from irregular daily work of up to twelve hours. None the less, Joey was pleased with the photo and thanked the photographer when he paid its cost; two dollars script.

Thankful that his stay under the photographer's tent was physically warming, Joey ventured back out into the weather on the mall and resumed his "strolling down the mall" persona. He again noted there was a definite shortage of young females about. Matter of fact, Joey concluded; if it were not for the female family relations of the tent entrepreneurs, there'd be no women present on the mall; …at all. This piqued Joey's interest since the MPs let him know there were several tents specializing in prostitution located near the Southern mall end point. 'There'd be women there!' he concluded.

He continued on his way to the South, and had to elbow his way past a group of loudly talking American soldiers. "Funny." He thought. "There's a lot more Americans on the mall now than when I started a half hour or so ago." And there were. There were now many American, British, Turkish and South Korean uniformed soldiers plus lesser numbers of US sailors …and merchant seamen on the mall. No matter its shortcomings, this Mall was apparently the "happening liberty stop" in Pusan.

He hadn't walked but a minute or two since the "Photographer's Studio", when from the crowd out popped Big Tom and his Fireman, Stan. Tom started out with; "Stan and me just got relieved and are off watch, and thought we'd "*hit the beach*"…pun intended. So here we are, Joey. Any suggestions on where we're going from here on this cold-ass Beach Mall?" Joey responded with; "It's always good seeing you, Tom. Answering your question; I'm going to the Southern end of the Mall. Got it from the Gate MPs that there are a couple of cat-houses…er, I mean "cat tents" at that end…and I'm gonna visit one of 'em!"

With Joey's pronouncement they turned and, three abreast started into the wind, past two American MPs in a parked Jeep and down the now crowded Mall strip. Tom suggested they hit a restaurant first for; "… a little warmth and a bottle of beer". He got no argument and the three "Liberty ship seamen" ducked into a relatively large, permanently built "bar & grill" solid-structure. Anxious to get off the street, none of the three managed to "catch" the place's name upon entry. Joey thought; "No matter… we're on the inside, the fire is burning and we will be served beer and whatever."

The place was rapidly filling with uniformed customers. Joey thought; everyone had the same idea…get the hell out of the cold! Beers ordered, the three eased back into their chairs, loosened their jackets and let-in the warmth from the beer joint's large, hibachi-type, open fire pit. It just happened that they were seated relatively close to the fire …and the chill they had picked up walking the Mall, soon disappeared. They then were comfortable. Their conversation while light initially, turned to the SS MC GOWAN and dwelt upon the ship grounding and the upcoming move to a dry dock "somewhere"; and then…"fixing the bucket up". The closest "civilized country" is Japan; so a shipyard and dry dock there seemed the most likely spot to move the "…no fuel left in MC GOWAN" to. The trio settled on that scenario as the one that was most logical, hence, to be taken.

Moving back to the bar scene, as would happen when mixing beer with liberty, a fight soon erupted a bare two tables away from the trio. With an echoing; " Who the hell are you calling a son-of-a-bitch?" Sounds of chairs being pushed back over the hard wooden floor, then the sounds and sights of a fist fight permeated the bar room. Tom stood to better see the fight. He then moved quickly toward the fight and grabbed the apparently better fighter by the lapels of his jacket. Mumbling in a "stage whisper" he said; "Hey stupid! You're gonna attract MPs and they'll be busting up our liberty by gettin' us all back to the busses that brought us here. Then they'll be arresting you and your fighting shipmate here… and lock you both up for the evening. All that shit stinks! Now sit down and be good little boys." And then in a stage whisper said; *"And, if'n the MPs show, you just keep your mouths shut! You don't know nothin'! Get it? "* The "fighters" nodded.

If nothing else affected all present, Big Tom's size was numbing. Joey didn't think anyone would physically challenge the huge seaman. His affect on the two battlers was "instantly pacifying". Tom turned the man loose upon completing his remarks and returned to Joey and Stan.

Sure enough, two MPs soon entered the club on a run. Their eyes scanned the now-peaceful interior and they visibly relaxed. "Any trouble here?"; one of the MPs called out to the gathered drinkers. A few scattered "No's" was the response. "Good! Keep it that way..." were their parting remarks.

After the MPs left, Stan then said; "Hey. They can't be all bad. Heard it from the 4-8 Fireman that if'n you're out a bit past the 10 PM curfew, get yourself into a bar, then have the Bartender call the MPs. When they arrive, play dumb. Say something like; 'How *the hell am I supposed to get back to my ship now? Christ, it's after curfew! Go outside and be arrested? I don't think so! I don't want to spend the rest of this night in the clink. So, what do I do now?'* Heard that, after that tale of troubles, most MPs will give you a lift in their Jeep, right-on back to the ship." Joey mumbled his response which included the phrase; "...Think I'll be giving that approach a testing tonight. Gonna need that lift back to the ship and other than being cold riding in an open Jeep, that seems both like the way home and to keep from getting locked up." Tom and Stan smiled at Joey's announcement.

The three seaman ordered and drank another beer and Tom and Stan decided to do their shopping on their way back to the ship. Since it was already their watch-time they opted to return to the ship "right now" and relieve their "standbys". *"Get started with heel and toeing It"* was the way Big Tom put it. Joey thought it was definitely interesting that they had arranged with the 4 - 8 Watch for that watch to handle the first couple of hours of their 8 – 12 Watch. Why? Joey thought; "That move extended the liberty time for the Mid-Watch-standers and it made it easier for those on the Mid Watch to pay back the owed watch-time later on...so, it all made sense."

Joey continued on toward where he thought the prostitutes were tented on the Mall. He noticed the crowd of uniformed US military personnel was thinning out with his walking-trip South on the peninsular Mall...and those people that remained were those younger civilian "Korean toughs" dressed in NATO uniform items. Joey sarcastically wondered whether they might be on the hunt to augment their wardrobe from an unaware drunk or two here tonight. "In any case..." he resolved to not let his guard down. He was definitely not going to get drunk here in wartime Korea!

Joey "lucked-out" with his "prostitute for the evening". Why? It so happened that when he reached the first "Love Tent" with people outside there was a pimp-type who was talking to a youngish girl wearing the traditional Korean garb of a warm, buttoned down jacket with collar turned up to protect against the wind, a full length, flower print-covered skirt and fur-padded, calf-high boots. Her hat was the woven gray wool, pull down type… and it covered her ears. The girl was markedly good looking and alert in demeanor. She reminded Joey of the Pearl City Nisei lady he had made love to "back there in Hawaii". In fact, this girl so looked like that Hawaiian lady, he thought to himself; 'Wonder if these Koreans can tell themselves apart from the Japanese, or Chinese for that matter, and vice versa?'

Joey wasted no time in finalizing the price with the pimp, but when he reached for the girl she seemed reticent. The pimp rattled off some reassuring babble in Korean to the girl but her composure didn't change. It took Joey almost a minute's worth of smiles, introductory comments and softly spoken English to get her "comfortable" with the situation. She then didn't resist his light pull on her arm and followed Joey into the tent. Introducing himself as they entered the tent, he "met" Kim. Happily, there was an oil reservoir lamp lit in a corner of the tent and a centered, lit hibachi pot "cooking" with reddish, hot coals, alongside the covered mattress, which was on the ground.

Kim continued to look uncomfortable with what was happening and Joey thought that the total lack of privacy in the tent had her reluctant to shed her clothes with a man present. He raised the blanket to a height above his head and held it out as a shield to his vision… and he continued to display a smiling and reassuring composure. She took "the hint" and disrobed, wrapped herself in the blanket and went to lie down on the mattress. Joey took his time getting naked and was fastidious about properly folding his clothes and stacking them close to the hibachi. His "lady for the evening" was not ashamed to look at the naked Joey, and for some reason, that comforted him. He slid under the blanket and alongside her and when he rolled over toward her, his erection rubbed the front of her right thigh. She inhaled deeply when that happened and he, not wanting the emotional moment to pass, ran his hand over her left breast. Her nipple was hard. He lowered his mouth over her right nipple and softly sucked that nipple while his hand went to caress her "private parts". He knew she was "ready" and he was happy with that knowledge. He "took her" gently and she was a very responsive lover.

Copulation over, they lay side by side. Joey smoked a Camel. His partner did not smoke but looked his face over very carefully. Joey thought she didn't miss one detail of his features. While it was not early, Joey did not want this evening to end after he dressed, so he, by mostly sign language, asked if she was hungry and would like something to eat. Kim quickly agreed to have a late dinner with him.

Joey gave little thought to her pimp and that man's possible reactions to Joey and the girl going to a close-by, available restaurant. The two "recent lovers" just left the tent and without any comment to him, went into a nearby Korean local "Kimchee emporium". Joey ordered for both of them. The grilled "liberated" Spam and kimchee he ordered promised to go well with a hot green tea and maybe a touch of pastry for desert. He was not disappointed. The main course food was delicious if a touch salty! His lady ate lustily, as if it might've been her first meal of the day.

Joey thought the late dinner with the girl was a fitting end to his first Pusan, South Korea, liberty. He escorted his "dinner date" back to her tent. Her pimp made his appearance at the tent entrance flap upon her entry, but seeing him this time had little effect on her demeanor. Kim's farewell to Joey was a warm hug and a kiss full on the lips. He hugged her back and took his time in releasing her. He turned on his heel at that point and headed back to where the busses parked.

It seemed to him most of the cold wind had died off and in the calm, cool air the walk back was almost comfortable. With the darkness, ambient light was virtually nonexistent. It was pitch black if one was not under the lighting of a place of business, so Joey watched his footing on the stone and dirt path. As he passed the photography shop he touched his pocket assuring himself that the photograph that was taken of him was still in his possession. It was. The candy vendor was still at his prior location selling his sesame seed and honey candy bars and "good customer", Joey bought his second candy bar of the evening.

He recalled he had threatened to parlay some lies into a free ride home by the MPs…but on second thought, he'd save that con for a different night. Now, all he wanted was to get back to the MC GOVERN and take his night watch. Of interest to him was the knowledge that it still was early enough that the curfew was not yet in effect! He had done a lot and it was still "early"!

He climbed aboard the bus displaying the sign "Pusan Harbor" as its destination. He checked his front right hand pocket for his Merchant Marine ID card. It was there and could be shown if needed. He did not plan on making any "touristy stops" on his way back to the Liberty ship and indeed, was somewhat in a hurry to get there…watch or no watch. On the ride "home" he noted the bus was passing through a "retail shopping" area of Pusan. He had not noticed this shopping area on his way to the Beach, but was quite happy it was there. He decided to return to this area the following morning, before his Noon to Four PM Watch. That stop was to be a "replacing consumables errand" stop. He needed *replacement* stockings, under ware and he harbored the thought he should buy a "nice" shirt or two to wear on liberty both here and in Japan. He also thought he'd ask his watch mate, Slim, to accompany him in the morning. He rationalized that "shopping", per se, *as defined by Slim's wife*, should not be "off-limits" for him.

The remainder of the ride back to the Harbor and his ship was uneventful. Checking his watch, he saw that he could be shifted into watch-standing attire prior to 11 PM and that was "fine with him". Passing the little, forlorn-looking Catholic Church raised that same question in him it had when he first saw it. *What in hell was it doing here in Korea and at the Harbor entrance?* No answer entered his mind.

Free of the bus and after exchanging a few pleasantries with the MPs at the Gate, Joey wasted no time in climbing the gangway to the ship's Main Deck. Once on deck, he took the time to check the Fuel Oil Manifold and the two portable FO tanks that were on service to feed the boilers. All appeared to be in order…and he saw that the Watch Oiler, Big Tom, was checking the deck cargo winch machinery. Aside from the ship listing slightly toward the sea wall, the overall "picture of absolute normalcy" for in-port, night watch-standing was satisfying to Joey.

A quick stop at the Engine Mess Hall for a fruit juice drink and sandwich brought him face to face with Slim. After exchanging "…what did you do on Liberty…?" with Slim, Joey suggested the shopping plan for the following morning and Slim jumped at the idea, saying; "Y'all know ah need lots of stuff for when we get to Japan an' dry dock. While ah could probably wait 'till we get to Japan to buy the stuff ah needs, Pusan's got to be as low costin' as Japan an' iffn they got what ah needs, buying here is as good as buyin' dere. Sure to have a few cold days an' in dry dock, ah won't be able to snuggle up to de boilers to keep warm. A couple of long sleeve items to wear are in the cards, an' dats fo' sho'."

Finished with his snack, Joey turned and headed into the 12 to 4 Watch berthing space. Slim was close behind. Joey changed clothes and was ready and in the Mess when Big Tom arrived to wake the 12 -4, relieving watch. While he still had almost a half hour before he was required to, for some reason Joey wanted to "relieve" Tom right then and there. He asked Tom if he had made the topside Oiler Rounds for the hour and Tom responded; "No. Ain't got around to it yet." Joey told Tom; "Ok, I've got the Watch and make the rounds… and you're relieved." Tom nodded in acknowledgement. Joey immediately went out on deck and checked the steam driving units on all the cargo winches. All were given a lathering of cylinder oil and graphite grease …and Joey could swear they ran better with the extra lubricants. They didn't but Joey was positive that they did.

Joey felt some "rumbling" in his stomach but felt the discomfort would pass and tried to ignore it. Stomach problems not-with-standing, the watch ran well for Joey, and with the Main Engine quiet, there really wasn't too much to do down in the plant. On his 2 AM topside round Joey saw the Junior Third Assistant hauling around his bottles of ammonia and Freon 12 gas. He asked the man if he needed some help with the "Refer Plants". The Junior Third responded with; "Always can use some help. And you can start with taking one of these bottles from me and carry it up to the Reefer Flats." Joey took the bottle off the Junior's left shoulder and mumbled; "Let's go…" Hefting the bottle, he really felt his stomach acting up with indigestion and felt he was "bloating" as well.

As with the last time Joey helped the Junior while on his 12 – 4 Watch, Joey contacted his Watch Engineer via the "Sound Powered Phones", and got permission to "…assist; but don't miss a Topside Round to do it!." The Junior told Joey to tell the Second; "*The Junior copies all* and Joey won't miss a thing regarding the watch." Joey relayed the reassurance.

At the "reefer flats" the Junior determined that the plant that uses ammonia as the refrigerant for the cargo hold cooling system (to circulate cold salt water to the cargo-hold cooling coils) was going to need some "serious work" when the MC GOWAN goes into dry dock. In the interim, a new seal was installed on the compressor…and fingers were crossed that;"*That part replacement will work to correct plant operation in the near term."* The Junior mentioned he'd get with the Chief Engineer and brief him on the issue after breakfast.

Because of the relative ease of the repair work he had done, Joey's confidence rose and he felt that when it came to servicing Liberty ship refrigeration and cooling systems, he was almost up to the task "Right now!" This was irrational thinking. He was nowhere close to having the know-how or experience to handle the job…or even to pass the Coast Guard vetting exam on the subject. With the Junior Engineer leaving the space, Joey immediately got on the sound powered phone with the Second and let him know he was going to take another Topside Round and then return to the Engine Room.

While all was running smoothly with the watch duties, Joey's stomach was now giving him real problems. On the way to the Engine Room he detoured to a "head" (bathroom) and vomited. He hoped this belly-emptying action would help him return to "normal". He mentally eliminated all sources of his discomfort except the final plate of kimchee he had with the girl. He wasn't clear on what actually constituted "stomach poisoning", which also could've come from the sesame bars, but didn't discount the kimchee, thinking; "Hell! I just might have a case of the runs from that crap." Returning to the Engine Room and still with an hour of watch to go, Joey let the Second know he had stomach problems…but could finish his watch. The Second responded with; "Just as soon as we get off watch, we'll get you some paregoric for your gut. That should do the trick… If not, you're just going to have to rely on puking that stuff up. Also, if you start running a fever, I'll send you to that waterfront First Aid Clinic that's aft of the ship, on the dock. I'll also get the word to the Chief and the Skipper for them to make log entries on your problem. In the meantime I think the *Manual* calls for you to drink lots of water. That normally helps with everything."

Joey finished his Watch, accompanied the Second to the Sick Bay, had his dose of paregoric and went on deck for the night air breeze… and the ability to "upchuck" over the side if need be. He estimated that his stomach clearing events to this point were probably all that he would need, and by the way, the paregoric appeared to be working. He was feeling better, and thinking he had; '…*probably not "severe" stomach poisoning, after all.*' He was correct in this analysis. He also thought; 'Might even be able to eat a bit of breakfast, if I let the greasy stuff alone'. Joey was on the mend!

Kim and the first night liberty actions indelible in his memory, Joey opted that other than making the shopping trip with Slim, to stay aboard their remaining two nights in Pusan. Joey thought it interesting that the war needs outpaced any thoughts of "laying down on the job" when it came to offloading the MC GOWAN. It took only three days! The Skipper had the word put out that the ship would be sailing for Japan in the evening of the third day…and; "All hands will be fully supportive of this scheduling!" The crew *fully supported the schedule!" All were "fully" ready for the change of venue!*

CHAPTER SEVENTEEN

NEXT STOP; ONOMICHI

Full portable fuel oil tanks firmly strapped to the deck forward of the amidships house, the SS MC GOWAN, with harbor tug assist, cleared her wharf mooring and pointed the Harbor Entrance. The day was clear and the "Ahead Slow" bell seemed adequate for clearing the Harbor… and also encouraging, was that the lightened ship responded to her rudder nicely. The tug was cast off…but continued astern, trailing the Liberty ship. While now underway, the Maneuvering Watch was kept on in case the ship had to anchor, so Joey stayed on the Fantail, on his station, while MC GOWAN was heading for the breakwater marking the Harbor exit.

Enroute to open water, Joey had a fine opportunity to see where he was when on the Beach Mall that first night. From the current one mile "track distance" to the peninsular, the Mall wasn't impressive. Though he tried to see the tent where he and Kim had their tryst, from this distance he couldn't recognize the "distinguishing features" of that "one girl, House of Ill Repute".

Joey took as a memory-jog his current view of the Mall, to recall just how "seedy" that piece of real estate looked from the deck of the Liberty; "… on this fine day." Contrarily, his thoughts of Kim were very positive and buoyed him in his overall recollections of being on liberty in Pusan.

Joey eased up to the two deck seamen who were on the fantail with him and asked; "Either of you two guys looking forward to visiting

Japan? Think it'll be as good as, or better than Pusan?" The younger of the two allowed that this was his first trip to the Western Pacific so he really didn't have an opinion regarding the question Joey asked. The older of the two said; "I guarantee Japan will be better... Most *bang for the buck* in the Pacific; no pun intended. While I don't think there's a soul on board that's been to Onomichi specifically, *the town is in Japan* and that's enough for all the crew I've talked to. They're just happy we're goin' there. Me, for one; I'm also happy we're goin' there!" Joey let all further conversation on this topic die. He had previously heard all this; "...Japan is a great place for seamen's liberty! Can't beat it anywhere in the Pacific!" ...and all such opinionating. He dropped the conversation with the deck hands and decided to rely on his own future Japanese "liberty experiences" for his take on the comparative value of them.

The first morning... after getting underway from Pusan the ship took a Southerly heading. Joey had made the early breakfast at 6: 30 AM and was now watching the passage of the Eastern shores of Kyushu in the dawn lighting. He could also see the faint Western edges of the major Japanese island of Honshu to the East...and it was almost directly under a rising sun. Joey thought; "Looks kinda like the Japanese flag." Not visible yet to Joey but also to the East, was the city of Hiroshima... which was located on the western tip of Honshu.

On its southerly heading, the Liberty was "dropping down" between the Honshu and Kyushu coasts. Joey recalled that the town of Onomichi was located in the Hiroshima Prefecture region and most of the Town was actually positioned on a small coastal island just to the south of Hiroshima. Joey would have to wait until the ship rounded the point of land to the South, before he'd be able to see Onomichi. He meant to remain on deck to do just that!

While winds and currents were benign, Joey, on deck, felt the vibrations of the reciprocating Main Engine, stop. This was disconcerting! This was *not good news* to the experienced "Watch-standing Oiler" that Joey had become. He immediately made his way down to the Operating Platform in the Engine Room to see if he could "help" there if *a serious problem* had caused the Engine shutdown. He found out that the main shaft to the propeller had a shaft journal bearing that was "heating up" and that was what caused the shutdown.

Joey knew that a "hot" shaft bearing was a very rare event. Joey wasted no time in getting started thinking as to "why" it happened. He immediately zeroed in to a shaft misalignment since the ship had run aground, changed her cargo status, and had taken damage to her "backbone", the keel. That "ship warping" incident alone could affect the shaft alignment. He coupled that with the total unloading in Pusan of the ship's deck and hold-carried cargo. That "dead weight" removal would also affect the ship's centers of buoyancy and gravity...and put keel bending and unusual "force moments" on the ship in general. *All of these situational forces could result in shaft misalignment.* Upon arrival in the plant Joey immediately asked if he could be of any help to the watch standers in handling "the fix".

In response to Joey's question, the Watch Engineer, the First Assistant, told Joey to get a gallon can of "light Gyro Oil" into the shaft alley and start injecting the oil into the shaft bearing "...to cool that bearing down." and allow the ship to resume her transit. Joey left the Operating Platform to do that, and in the interim, the on-Watch Oiler had the sea water spigot to the bearing's "upper housing" opened and cut-in. Joey knew that spilling water over the bearing's upper shell was really the best (early) method of cooling the bearing. If cut in early enough in the emergency, that water could stave off completely, or, at least minimize damage to the shaft bearing's Babbitt surfaces.

Using the back of his hand to monitor the heat in the bearing, Joey carefully applied the gyro oil to the oil reservoir of the upper bearing shell. He felt the bearing cooling down and after another fifteen minutes of monitoring, throttled down the cooling water. After the Engineer returned the engine to its normal steaming turns of 76 RPM, Joey noted the bearing appeared to have nicely survived the slight heat-up, was remaining cool and was not contributing to any shaft vibration. The fast action taken by all in the Engine Room was noted by the Chief Engineer and he shouted to all from the Operating Platform; **"Kudos to all...and thanks!"**

The remainder of the transit to Onomichi was uneventful. The Skipper had planned to make it to the dry dock in the town by early afternoon...and "be on the blocks" by sunset. The hot journal bearing slowed the time for docking down by a couple of hours...so Joey was off watch when the ship was in the early stages of preparing to and then lining up to enter the dock. He went topside to the portside aft, to, as was becoming a habit, play "tourist"... while also being a member of the Number 4 Line handling team.

By glancing to the West (his left), he saw a full baseball diamond coming into view around a point of flat land near the town's Southern sea shore. This diamond came complete with home-run-outfield fencing, high fencing behind the batter's box, complete player-dugouts, white baselines, a ready-to-go pitcher's mound and two sets of observer-stands. He thought; "Holy smoke! I didn't know the Japanese were into baseball."

For some reason, he really had not known that the Japanese were almost as fanatic as most Americans were about baseball. Since he had played as a catcher in New York's Police Athletic League, on sandlots and in high school, he immediately gave thought to having a ship's team formed. If that happened, maybe they'd be able to get in a game or two with "the locals" while the ship was in dock. He noted he had neglected to bring any baseball equipment with him to the Liberty ship... and was certain no one else in the crew did either. Almost like underscoring the fact that Joey's rambling thoughts about baseball didn't matter, the ship continued on its Northerly leg...the dry dock was dead ahead.

Now looking ahead while the ship was approaching the after wall of the dock, and then watching the docking pilot minutely align the ship with the dock centerline, Joey was looking forward to observing a flawless overall alignment of the ship with the dock's keel blocks.

At the same time he was able to see a relatively large chunk of the downtown area of Onomichi fanning out on both bows. He saw the shops, restaurants and what appeared to be schools and other public buildings that made up the town, but from his vantage point on the ship, he had to look up the hill, to find dwellings. The streets feeding the residential area, like latitude lines on a chart, horizontally circled the hill front. Also chart-like, the Avenues, like longitude lines, were slightly offset from the vertical, but tied the streets together. The buildings in the entire residential area were single-storied and in the early evening light, looked spotlessly clean.

Noting the dichotomy with the appearance of the city-scape they had just departed, Joey came to the finding; 'There's a big difference between this town and Pusan, Korea … with Onomichi being the winner; since it was just plain clean!'

CHAPTER EIGHTEEN

DRY DOCKING

As noted, the ship proceeded to the open dock entrance and "lined its centerline up" with the "dock's navigation range". It is to Joey's credit that other than just standing by the after line, he was able to watch, and from a technical standpoint, the entire "ship handling drill" to line MC GOWAN up with "the blocks" that awaited its keel and bottom. While it, the alignment, took time, Joey thought the operation went smoothly…and he was thinking correctly! It only took about a half hour for the ship to be properly lined up, and the dock's doors shut. There were four diver-tending, small boats with the Liberty inside the dry dock.

It was then that Japanese salvage divers in modern wet suits and fed air from barge mounted air-compressors, dropped into the water to inspect and "chart" the ship's bottom damage. The pertinent information they obtained during their dives was passed to the Japanese Docking Pilot and he directed which keel blocks to be slightly repositioned to allow for the ship's damage. The Japanese did this using the chain falls hooked to those blocks to be moved. Divers checked the final block locations for accuracy in their placement.

Following that block repositioning, the Docking Pilot passed the word to the dock engineers to start pumping out the sea water and thus, lower the Liberty on to the blocks. It was then that the older AB on watch aft with Joey, advised all within earshot that; "My hat is off to the Japanese for their ability to properly place this Liberty on the blocks considering the damage she took to her bottom plating when she grounded. Wonder if they'll be able to work on and fix the entire bottom with this one block placement." Joey took this comment "on board"... and found he shared the AB's "Wonder if..." He decided at that time to visibly check on this bottom damage versus block placement at his earliest opportunity.

The ship wasn't on the blocks and the sea water drained to just inches and puddles for fifteen minutes when the Japanese "Riggers" had a companionway in place on the ship, aft of the house, leading to the Dock's second deck, or one deck down from the Upper or Main Deck of the Dock. This was a "graving dock", or was actually a hole in the land so its internal ladders and passageways had to be followed for anyone to eventually make it down to the ship's keel area on the dock's base, or down to the hard earth on the Town-side.

With the companionway in place, Joey opted to make it into Town that evening for his evening meal and to just "stretch his legs on solid land" for a few hours. With the ship on the blocks and the Maneuvering Watch secured, Joey made his way into the Engine Room to help with the securing of the plant and the hook-up of all dock-supplied ship's services for electrical power, fresh water and sewage removal-housekeeping services. Pallets for stacking garbage and other waste containers were placed on the ship's deck immediately to starboard of the mid-ships house.

The Engineer on Watch directed Joey to check on the Steering Engines to insure they were put to sleep properly, and then to hook-up the dock-provided water to the Shaft Seal and Bearing to keep its Lignum Vitae wood (bearing material) segments from drying and shrinking during the docking period. Joey did as directed and then made it up to his sleeping quarters to shed work clothes in favor of those duds chosen for liberty. Slim was already there and in bed without shoes, but not yet asleep. Joey greeted Slim upon his entry and invited Slim along with him on liberty...and possibly for a meal that they could try "on the beach" (when ashore). Slim said that securing the boilers, feed water and the Main Steam systems : "...pooped me out! Thank ah'll git supper on board, n'den crap out early. We gonna be in dis dock for a few weeks so ah'll have plenty o'time to become an expert on all thangs dat Onomichi has t'offa."

Joey noted aloud that Slim was doing some "smart thinking" in staying on board, him being married and all. He said; "Do some eating for me at supper! And, if you do decide to hit the beach later, at least have the stew burner leave sandwich material for me, "the liberty hound", for when I come back aboard for my Watch. Joey then exited his quarters and made for the stern companionway then ashore...thinking; 'Exploring the dry dock flooring arrangements will just have to wait. The time for liberty is now!'

CHAPTER NINETEEN

WHAT'S IN ONOMICHI?

Joey was surprised at how much walking and ladder-negotiating was involved in getting free of the dry dock. There was no English speaking security watch other than an AB Watch stander on the ship so the trip out of the dock, for Joey, was done in silence. He was surprised that the pathway leading from the base of the (dock) steps to the nearest Onomichi street was paved with close fitting and small cobble-stones. At about 4:30PM he knew he was very "early" in departing the ship. He noted with interest that there was already a "taxi", of sorts, waiting for its first "American seaman fare".

The taxi was tiny,… a little more than a metal and glass covered three-wheel motor bike, called a "Toyopet",… and was built by the Toyota Motor company. If they weren't physically too large, two passengers could be seated in the cab's rear seat. Joey, using all ten fingers for counting, ascertained the price for a ride into the geisha house district of town was 350Y; …or almost a dollar at the 360Y per script dollar Exchange Rate that was dictated by the "MacArthur Occupation" administration. As in South Korea, Mac Arthur was the "dude in charge" in Japan.

Joey did not react adversely to the stated cab fare but opted not to take the Toyopet. It was too beautiful an evening to do anything but walk to anyplace in the close-in, intermediate, bordering town. With his back to the harbor, Joey headed directly for the base of the hill that was the backdrop for the lower, waterfront neighborhoods that surrounded the dry dock on three sides. This hill seemed to vertically end in a tightly knit crown of trees; or orchard that was just above the residential area.

The vertical climb from the waterfront to where, he was advised, the Geisha Strip was located, was evaluated as "moderate" and the Strip was located immediately below the orchard. In either case, the climbing route followed the main avenue up the hill, which he estimated to boast a 10% grade. With this moderate grade, Joey felt he should've had little trouble negotiating it.

Joey indeed, did climb it, but after months of physically restrictive "shipboard living", the climb came with some difficulty. Joey had a goal for this climb and that goal was to reach a very large bar he could see from the dock. Twenty minutes after starting from the dry dock, Joey was entering the "large bar"…and this "bar spot" was still two blocks short of and downhill of the "orchard". The name of this bar was the "Sakura", and it was written in both the simple "sound oriented" Japanese Khana alphabet and in English lettering. Joey later asked for the translation of the name into English and was told it was "Cherry Blossom".

Even after a minute or two, on entering the bar, Joey, at this level above the waterfront, was still breathing somewhat heavily from the exertion of the climb. At the door, the middle-aged, male owner of the bar met Joey at the door and by gesturing, passed the message that Joey should remove his shoes prior to entering. Wearing clean and almost new socks, Joey readily complied. Upon Joey's entry, again relying on gesturing and pointing, the owner offered Joey a whiskey drink from a bottle on which a label was affixed advertising the contents as Suntory "Scotch whiskey". Joey knew that the whiskey was a product of Japan, not Scotland, but correctly deduced that the price per drink would be elevated by inclusion of the word "Scotch" in the branding of the liquor.

Alongside the Suntory Scotch, was a more modestly titled bottle of "Tory Whiskey". By receiving the answer to the question of relative cost between the two, Joey settled on a drink made with the Tory whiskey, which was about 50% the cheaper.

Joey had not been in the bar ten minutes when in came two ladies in ornate, with gold thread inlays, kimonos (robes) and silver thread inlayed obis (sashes), powdered faces, upswept and shiny, black hairdos with wooden pins running through the folds of hair,… and white, split toed foot coverings. Their wooden shoes (getas) were left at the bar doorway's wooden storage platform for shoes. Joey had previously heard of ladies dressed in traditional garbs, like these that the girls had on, while he was still in Brooklyn, and that knowledge helped him identify them as geishas. He had also heard that these geishas were expert in making men comfortable …whether the men were engaged in social drinking or just having a relaxing meal. Their abode was named by Westerners; "Geisha Houses", so Joey concluded that he had found his first Geisha House.

His prior knowledge included that these young women were, for the most part, "sold into" the geisha business by their families, most with their fathers making the decision.

Indeed the Sakura Bar was Joey's first Geisha House experience and that fact caught and kept his interest. He suspected that the geishas were not prostitutes and subsequently found that thought to be accurate. Going along with the attention the two ladies were placing on him, he found that one of them was taking the lead in assuring his drink glass was filled and that he was kept comfortable. After just a few minutes the second geisha bowed, said what he thought to be "Koban wa" (which he later determined to be a late-evening "goodbye" in Japanese) and left the open bar area for an enjoining room.

He was on his second whiskey when three middle aged Japanese men entered the House and were warmly greeted by the owner. The "second" geisha reappeared and proceeded to care for these men. The owner then got on the telephone, and in a whispering conversation with someone, who Joey surmised was something of a "geisha agent", attempted to get other geishas to come to work; …as his place of business was getting busy.

CHAPTER TWENTY

A GEISHA FRIEND

After his asking, Joey's companion gave him her name; Kozuko Minori. It took Kozuko a few tries before she pronounced "Joee" as he wanted. It was interesting that something as simple as an introductory name exchange was able to get both Kozuko and Joey giggling, but that is what happened. Further she conveyed the thought that the two of them were "friends" or; Tomodachi ("friend" in Japanese) was the descriptive name she placed on Joey.

While conversing with her, Joey "measured" Kozuko against the oriental ladies he had become acquainted with during the port visits the MC GOWAN had made since leaving Beaumont. Joey quickly came to the conclusion that younger "Oriental" ladies were sturdily built, boasted an average height that was some six inches shorter than he was, had, dark to almost black eyes and hair, and had a Chinese-like, high cheek-boned, "Oriental look and color" to them. He had mentally combined into one thought the Hawaiian, Nisei lady, he met at the Pearl City Tavern with the Korean girl, Kim, and now, the Japanese geisha lady, Kozuko. These three young women "comprised his knowledge of Oriental ladies".

Rethinking the issue, he again came to the conclusion that their features, hair and skin color all were nearly identical! To him, they really did all look alike. Further, to Joey's Western perception, he thought; *they all could have been sisters.* As he observed in Korea, he again concluded that because of their physical similarities, these women would not know each other's Asian country of origin if, language aside, and as strangers, they were introduced to each other.

Joey still had had nothing to eat since he got off Watch...and was somewhat hungry. With now casual gesturing, he asked Kozuko if the bar served any food. Her response required that she make a trip to the owner for an answer to the question. Joey did not understand their conversation, but the owner did go into a back room and return with a jar of soy sauce, a covered platter of breaded shrimp, rice cakes and a metal cooking grill to be placed above the burning coals of the hibachi that Joey and Kozuko had been sharing for warmth.

Kozuko took the food and cooking supplies to the area where their straw mats were and then went back to the bar owner for a tray containing a lacquered jar of saki rice wine and two small, similarly lacquered cups. Joey knew well that Kozuko was preparing to make and serve him his dinner and asked her in sign language if she wanted money to pay the owner for the food and drink,... and also for her "company". Kozuko responded with "Ie!" (No!); and also pointed to her wrist, as if she had a watch on, and gestured that his "paying later-on" would be fine.

The breaded shrimp cooked nicely on the hibachi and while they were cooking Kozuko kept his saki cup filled. The saki did not taste like any western wine he had previously, but went quite well with the breaded, grilled and dipped in soy sauce... shrimp. He asked what this food was called in Japanese and was told it was "tempura" (or breaded and grilled food). The rice cake was "gohan" and/or "ohagi" (Japanese for just plain "rice" and/or "sweetened rice ball").

Upon finishing his meal, he patted his stomach and gave the expression of being "full". This wasn't a lie. He was satiated and the never-ending cups-full of warm saki were beginning to make him sleepy. In the light wood and paper walled-off room he and Kozuko occupied, there was still enough visibility through the partially open doorway for them to be able to see the arrival and departure of any other customers to the House. Joey saw a youngish Japanese man in work clothes consisting of jacket, chino pants and shirt and high-top, laced boots arrive and get into a short conversation with the owner. He never removed his shoes so the two talked on the step leading in to the bar.

Overhearing scraps of the conversation between the proprietor and the working man, Joey thought he heard the name "kozu-chan" (a nickname for the formal: "Kozuko san", or "Miss Kozuko") mentioned more than once. The young man got visibly upset when the owner did not produce "Kozu-chan" and then gestured for the fellow to leave his establishment.

During this episode, that was happening just outside of their room, Kozuko whispered to Joey the man's name; Akio. Joey nodded and questioning, whispered back to her; "Friend?" ("Tomodachi?") She nodded and said *"Hai, aijin."* (Yes, boyfriend.). Joey then knew she had a lover-boyfriend, and this guy was the "boyfriend"…and probably had a short temper. Joey tried to put the man out of his mind with the thought; "…that he and Kozuko only had a dinner together that she served and prepared …" and also that *Kozuko was really in the "service or waitress business"* as a working geisha. Joey thought that she was just doing her job…and that he was just her customer. His final thought on the subject however, was that; "It would've been much better if Akio had never shown up, 'cause now I've got to watch my back."

Their farewell, though somewhat strained by Akio's appearance, had settled on the facts that he, Joey, would return to her in the future … and that he and she were indeed "tomo-dachi's". Joey found that he "liked" this girl and looked forward to his return to the Sakura Bar and to her.

CHAPTER TWENTY ONE

A Ship's Baseball Team?

His downhill walk back to the waterfront from the "Geisha House" was much easier on him than his trip up. He did spend some effort on checking the shadows along the way to see if Akio had "hidden out to waylay, with a planned attack on him".

The walk through the darkened and quiet town turned out to be uneventful. From his elevated view while descending through the residential area, the dry dock was his visual guide back. With this lighted, hence highly visible target, the night trip was made easy. He saw the MC GOWAN on blocks in the dock, and it was that location, the occupied portion of the dock, that was brightly lit for the night work… that now was ongoing. He had to shield his eyes when welding arcs flared and also later, when he was closer to the dock and the cutting torches caused "spark showers".

To get to the dry dock he also had to pass a few of the town's places of business and one of them was a modest establishment that sold athletic equipment. He stopped in front of that store and squinted through the window to see, if he could, the advertised "athletic gear". Further, as if reading his mind, while unlit, the sign over its door was still quite readable and had some of the athletic (baseball equipment) items listed under two column headings; one column in khana-written Japanese, the other in English. Joey noted that "baseball" had a Japanese name of "yakyu" and that the gear; the gloves and bats in the window display all looked like they were imported from America. He did not see any horsehide baseballs. He thought; '… no matter, in spite of "a Japanese name like yakyu", baseball was still baseball!' Joey looked at the catcher's mitt in the window and his mind carried him back to his own ball-playing days, spent almost totally as a "catcher".

His viewing the store window-front succeeded in getting his mind off of Kozuko and Akio… and in getting him to thinking that; with perhaps the ship spending up to a month in the Onomichi dry dock, perhaps a ship's baseball team might really be '…in the cards. Unlikely to happen, but it's a thought.' He then turned to the dry dock siding and the Liberty ship beyond.

With the hammering and other metal work on the ship's bottom going on almost non-stop, sleeping in the ship was a chore for the entire ship's company. Upon his return, Joey tried to, but was unsuccessful, in getting a needed nap prior to his assuming the mid-watch. It seemed to him that the dock workers were taking some sort of sadistic pleasure in keeping him awake. A trip across the passageway into the mess deck for a cigarette and a bite to eat were intended to substitute for the unattainable sleep. He had forgotten about Slim and was almost surprised to see him at the mess table with a "mystery-meat" and American cheese sandwich and glass of green "bug juice".

"Hey Slim… you can't sleep either?" Joey started with…then continued; "You play any baseball back when you were younger? … What with the ball Park around the hill from this dock and even closer, the right handy sports equipment store I saw this evening, I think the Gods are wanting us to put a team together and play the local Japanese squad. Think it'll be fun…"a gas", actually. And it would be a super way to help us spend some of our "free time" during the next few weeks we'll be in this dock."

While Joey was catching his breath after this monologue, Slim got this weird look on his face; smiled and said; "Yeah. Played first base an' did sum pitchin' in ha-school…but den let it all go when ah lef' to go to sea sum six or so years ago. Probably could maybe get back in sum sorta shape if'n we start a team. Don' know about bein' a pitcher…though. (Pause) Y'all thank y'can make it work?"

110

Joey came back with; "All I know is that the Japanese name for baseball is *yakyu,* and with the presence of the field, equipment and enough local, young guys to play, they probably already have some sort of local team and "B-ball league" that they're proud of. So, with us USA-types as "the enemy", they would jump at the chance to kick our "war winning" butts. By the way, *you and I are probably not the only dudes on this bucket to have played some ball so I think a hell-of-a-lot more of our guys will also jump at a chance to swing a bat.* Think it's a "natural" and going to happen…and if we can get some relief with the Watch requirements, it'd be a "go". Now, *it's up to us to make sure it happens!*

Tomorrow, I'm gonna see if I can find the dude on the beach who's their manager …or who talks for the local team, and then do some exploring. Also, think I'll be getting a price listing on the ball gear, caps and shoes we'll be needing. Hey, …wanna come along with me on this, after breakfast, shopping trip? …You know? All this steaming we've done has me with a roll of bucks in my pocket…and I'm looking for a place to get rid of some of that cash." Slim, still smiling, added; "Shore! If'n we hit dat store, ma bet is dat the guy runnin' it will be able to answer all your queshuns."

The two watch-mates went back to their quarters and now, had no trouble falling to sleep. Seems the "baseball mission" they just signed-up-to took the place in their brains that had, here-to-fore, concentrated on the ship-repair noise emanating from the hull.

Their mid watch came and went without the normal items of engineering interest being checked-on by the Watch Oiler and Fireman. Those main engine and auxiliaries checks were not needed while the ship was in dock and on the blocks. Instead, the Chief Engineer dictated that the Watch people would work on "keying up" and/or replacing the Main Engine and shaft bearing's babbitted surfaces. In Joey's thoughts, this work was simply; an overhaul of the engine.

CHAPTER TWENTY TWO

"Time Out" for Overhaul

When Joey and Slim made it down to the Lower Level they found spread out on the deck plates the bearing components plus heavy hand and machine tools to disassemble, scrape and fit the bearing halves. Big Tom knew that Slim had prior experience with "overhauling a Liberty's reciprocating, main engine" and would impart the required knowledge related to that task to Joey, and so did not elaborate on what awaited them below, but just gave the two mid-watch-standers a shake to wake them, with the comment; "Dress for dirty work!" and an offhand remark about "...see you down in the hole, soon".

The entire environment in the ship and dry dock was one of cold dampness, a climate that fit the "early Spring time" they were in! It was very uncomfortable, so Joey and Slim dressed with sweat shirts and outer flannel shirts. Even after this care in clothes selected, it was still uncomfortably cold. After their stop in the Mess Deck for hot coffee and "a baked something-sweet", the two headed below into the plant.

At the operating platform they were greeted by the sight of the main engine in its "early overhaul" status. Chain falls were in place to "lift and support" the LP Unit's con-rod and wrist pin… so as to get at that unit's heavy bearings. After a fast check, Joey saw that all engine unit steam drains were in the "open" position and basically, dry. He also noted the "early" preparations for the overhaul, such as pulling the lubricating wicks leading from the LO pans, had been done. Since the engine's LP Unit was obviously being worked on, and no inadvertent engine movement was desired, Joey walked to it and visually checked the LP Unit cylinder drain and its discharge to the condenser for their being closed,…they were, and no steam was being applied to the engine.

The drains were almost dry and the condenser "was asleep,"…hence he deduced there was no steam remaining in the engine. He looked over to the boiler fronts and saw both boilers were secured and cooling down. While he did see a trickle of water seeping from the LPs lower-cylinder drain, it was minimal …and he knew that unit, like the IP and HP, was "safe" for disassembly and overhaul.

These checks really were "after-the-fact", since one of the engine's units was already partially disassembled and being worked on. Again, he didn't need to, but checked anyway to see the position of the engine's Reversing Gearing. It was "engaged" so Joey knew the engine, now locked, could not now have any unexpected shaft rotation from any source, and that also made him feel better. "The safety precautions were being followed."

With the reversing engine locked, and shut-down. Now he knew that someone (he), would be safe if there was a need to get into the engine's crank pit or climb-up one of the three con-rods or unit follower-guides. The bottom line was; he knew that the engaged jacking gear kept the engine from having any con-rod or crank shaft movement, …period! And that thought was comforting.

The Second Assistant and the Chief were the two "licensed" workers on the scene and they bore responsibility for the results. Because of this role they shared, they "directed worker traffic and efforts" on the flats. *At this time, Joey knew that the work on the LP Unit took their complete attention!*

With the chain falls supporting the weight of all the unit's moving parts, the upper-crank bearing half at the LP-end was being lifted by a separate "fall" for inspection. If its inspection so indicated that a minor adjustment was needed, shims would be installed or removed to obtain the proper clearances of the bearing's Babbitt-surfaces. In case of major wear, this contributed to the decision for refitting and reinstalling the existing bearing inserts, or go for new Babbitt bearing inserts.

For the key findings to support that decision, obtaining the "actual clearance measurements"; the Chief used thin "leads" that were to be to be strung across the bearing surface. These leads were crushed to existing (clearance) dimensions when the bearing was reassembled around the shaft. Then, when the shell was subsequently disassembled, the resulting "lead thickness" was micrometer-measured to check on the resulting running-space-clearance in the bearing. That measurement "specification" was in the "thousandths of an inch" range. Stating the procedure again, if the clearance was too large, brass shims would be removed to realize the desired clearance when reassembled. If too small (tight) a clearance resulted, shims were added or the bearing halves were scraped down to tolerance, by hand.

Recapping, Joey and Slim had relieved Big Tom and Stan in assisting the two engineers with their efforts. Work management, while using watchstanders, called for "day work procedures" which consisted of working for two hours straight then "coffee-braking" for a short coffee and cigarette break; then going back to work on the engine overhaul for the remaining two hours of the Watch. The engineers were taking the second "set of leads" on the LP Unit Crankshaft Bearing halves when it was time for Joey and Slim to be relieved. Upon their relief, they were surprised that for other than for some oil stains, they were relatively clean… further, with the "cool temperature" in the Engine Room, the two of them had not really broken a sweat!

It was still a couple of hours before breakfast would be available so Joey and Slim took showers, and remarked on how good the hot water felt. Also, since they didn't have "to make" the fresh water in the ships Evaporator Plant, the showers they took were indeed "luxurious" in water usage!

Their work on Watch had taken its toll. They were tired! Both Joey and Slim fell fast asleep following their showers and didn't make the breakfast sitting. They got up shortly before 9 AM and decided to have breakfast in town, do a bit of "looking around" and make it back by 11:30 for their watch. That schedule was tight but doable.

They quickly prepared to go ashore but knowing they would go right back on-watch, they didn't put on any "liberty-going" clothes. Clean "working duds" would have to do.

CHAPTER TWENTY THREE

BASEBALL? FOR SURE!

Leaving the dry dock on a beautiful morning had them both in good moods. They immediately circled back to where the sporting goods store was and went in to both browse and get answers to questions regarding a local Japanese baseball league that perhaps, the ship could participate in.

When the two "12 to 4 watch standers" made it into the sporting goods store, they met the proprietor; a one armed, middle-aged gent named *Sawada San*. While Slim "played with" a first baseman's mitt whose pocket he hit with his fist several times, Joey engaged Mr. Sawada on the details associated with local, Japanese baseball activities. Sawada San readily and smilingly responded to the Americans. In very poor English he conveyed to Joey that he'd have the coach/manager of the local team visit the ship to talk to Joey; and if he could, that man would answer Joey's questions.

With a heavy Japanese accent, the proprietor said; "Basebaur season soon to start...maybe one week befo' Cherry Brossom party-time. Think, he (the manager) be hoppy to meet with you now." Joey responded with; "Great! Have him make it to the ship around noon-meal-time, 11: 00 to 11: 30, in the Engineers' Crew Mess. Maybe I can get him a meal on his visit."

This preferred visit time was put forth by Joey since he and Slim would have to be on-watch starting at 11: 45, and this 11: 00 arrival would allow enough conversation to insure the major planning would be

116

completed for their participation in local ball games,… all before they had to leave to go on watch. Sawada San understood Joey completely and asked if this day was a good day for the visit. Joey nodded an emphatic "Yes!"

Sure enough, a youngish-looking Japanese, who spoke good, if accented English, arrived in the crew's Engineering Mess at 11:00. His name was Yoshio and he had a huge smile on his face during the introductions. When Yoshio was seated at his table, Joey asked Otis if he could intercede with the cook and get Yoshio a plate of food. The plate was immediately forthcoming, and it held a good-sized serving of the day's offering; Southern Fried Chicken, mashed Spuds and cooked Peas and Carrots. And Otis told Joey; it was "…with the cook's blessing, and our cook wants to know when we'll be playing our first game. He's an outfielder!"

Yoshio obviously appreciated the offer of food and just asked for some "*soyu*", soy sauce, to douse the chicken with and turn it into a "tempura look-alike". The knife and fork utensils were fine… and chop sticks (*o'hashi*) were not needed.

The two major planners; Joey and Yoshio, decided that there was no time better to make that first game happen, than making it happen real soon;… like this Saturday …in the morning at 10 AM. Ten O'clock was specifically chosen because the Japanese had another scheduled game that evening … and this game would make it a doable double-header-day for them. To further ease the scheduling impact on the Japanese team, which was named The Onomichi Giants, the game with the Americans was to be limited to seven innings.

Joey's baseball recruiting notes, posted in the Deck and Engine Messes, Wardroom and at the ship's companionway, were very effective in attracting seamen who had played ball previously to sign up as "interested, by position played", to being part of the ship's team. By the following morning, Tuesday, his listing was almost complete and other than having to shift a few names around to cover all "skilled positions", he knew he had enough players to field a team. Having a ship manned at 42 people, all who were relatively young males, helped.

It was to Joey's credit that he did not want the acquisition of uniforms and specialized gear like catchers protective equipment, gloves, mitts, bats and balls to be a prohibitive expenditure by the ball-playing, ship's seamen. Upon asking Yoshio, if the ship could use some of the Japanese gear, Joey received a big "thumbs-up" sign. That now kept the American player expenditure basically limited to buying a cap, a cup, athletic socks and cleated-shoes. *Definitely doable!*

Yoshio ate lunch and was escorted to the ship's companionway by Joey. Prior to the final goodbye, Joey confirmed the game time as 10 AM, Saturday…and then asked, as if as an after- thought, if the ship's team could borrow the ball gear on Thursday, at noon, to use in a practice session or two prior to the game. Joey was told; *"Hai!"* and the gear would be delivered to the ship by one of the three-wheeled Toyopet-trucks that frequented the dock entrance, at lunchtime Thursday… if the seamen could insure it all was delivered to the ball field Saturday morning. Joey allayed the manager's concern by pledging "the gear return as needed". The manager left the ship "all smiles!"

As planned, Joey had to wait until Thursday afternoon following lunch to get a majority of his ball players to make their first practice …with real honest-to-goodness ball gear. The field had dried out somewhat due to a lack of rain for almost a week, and was "fast" for the infield practice.

Only a handful of ball players had to practice without baseball shoes, and did some slipping around on the newly sprouting grass because of their lack of cleats. These players either had problems finding shoes that fit because their foot size exceeded the largest size shoes the sporting goods store stocked, or because they, the seamen, just delayed purchasing the baseball shoes for some other reason.

One large Texan AB even practiced without shoes. "Ah'm here an' wifout shoes 'cause ah loves baseball…even if ah hates dem slant-eyed, damn Japs!" was his introductory sentence to Joey. Before Joey had a chance to respond, Big Tom, who overheard the remark and who had attended a portion of the practice out of interest, even if he wasn't to play, "jumped on" the Texan with; "Hey stupid! We're the guests here, and we're not going to piss the locals off with your kind of Bullshit. You don't like the Japanese? Then get the hell off the team so you don't have a chance to screw this deal up for all of us. "Chastised", and with glove in hand, the Texan ran into the field without replying to Tom.

Joey, catching for Otis who, in turn, was trying to get back into some sort of a "pitching rhythm"; noted that, for this practice anyway, they were using hard rubber, serrated balls of the correct (horsehide baseball "regulation") size and weight. Otis observed that the serrations allowed this ball to break "like mad" when a curve was thrown. It took Joey quite a while before he felt comfortable catching for Otis and his "super-curves". They both had the opinion that the ball itself placed the projected outcome of the game even further into the realm of "guesswork". "We just might go hitless 'cause of that ball!" was Joey's final observation.

Two practices behind them, and all sorts of side-deals made to arrange for watch-standing reliefs also behind them; the American "team", attired with blue ball caps-sans-logo and with non-slip shoes of some sort, made the field by 9: 30 AM Saturday. They were afforded their choice of dugout and opted for the third base-line dugout to allow them a closer view of the majority of fans in the stands.

The Onomichi Giants followed the protocol of having the visiting ball club have the first at-bat. Joey, not knowing who the better hitters were at this stage of the game, set up a batting order with their largest and most muscular players making up the listing of "lead-off batters". Since short sleeve shirts were the shirts of choice in the warm, Spring weather, the comparatively large arm-muscles displayed by the Americans brought admiring "Oohs and Aahs" from the Japanese youngsters in the stands. On the other hand, *the hitting non-performance of the Americans*, against the monster-curves tossed at them by the Japanese pitcher, had the kids giggling!

It was "four up" to the plate "for three outs" in the top-of-the-First for the Americans. At third in the "order", swinging a bit late and dramatically choking up on the bat, Slim connected for a hit over the pitcher's head ... but was then left stranded there on First by a strikeout of the fourth batter, Joey.

Donning the borrowed catcher's chest protector, shin guards and face mask protector took Joey a while. He was a bit tardy in getting behind the plate for the bottom of the inning. He took three throws from Otis and signaled his being warmed-up to Otis, who then signaled his readiness to the Plate-Umpire…who yelled; **"PRAY BAUR"**! Summoning up his best and loudest, Brooklyn-voice, Joey set up a line of "chatter" from behind the plate to ostensibly support his pitcher, Otis. However, by his loudness, Joey also attracted the attention of the fans, who now filled the stands and were also numerously hanging onto the fences leading past the bases into the outfield.

Immediately, with the first pitch from Otis, Joey shouted; **"SWEENG BATTAH!"**…and the batter hesitated a moment, but then swung and missed. Catching the ball, Joey made a "thing" of getting up from his crouch and "showing the ball" to the batter…with the comment; "Ya gotta hit this thing…" The Japanese youngsters who probably had never before witnessed these antics from a catcher were highly amused, and by the end of the inning were repeating Joey's **"SWEENG BATTAH"** to all the Japanese players who were "taking" a pitch.

With the start of the ballgame, Joey was impressed with how Otis, with so little practice, had managed to control the serrated ball…and throw strikes. It was now totally up to Joey to "call for" the "correct pitch location" from Otis… and he got better with it as the inning wore on. The Japanese second batter in the order hit a single and with Joey struggling to handle the pitches from Otis, stole second… without even a toss from Joey to try to get him out. The big, shoeless Texan in Center Field yelled at Joey; "Hey catcher; throw the God-damn ball to Second…he's got me backing him up; …Damn it!" Joey raised his glove and simply waived in acknowledgement to the comment…and started his "chatter" again.

It was amazing that Otis was able to "hang-in there" pitching for inning after inning, but he did…and for all seven innings. Joey's **"SWEENG BATTAAH"** really caught on with the Japanese kids and was repeated by them for the entire game.

The game "went into the record books" as a 3 to 1 victory for the local, Onomichi Giants. The seamen participating in the game, and those just there to watch the action, thoroughly enjoyed "the baseball-break" from ship's work in the dry dock. Further, the "watchers" happily crowded around the ball players coming out of the dugout to give them pats on the back and words of appreciation for their efforts.

The Japanese team with Yoshio, the Baseball Coordinator, leading, crowded around the ship's team immediately following the final out. They then formally presented Joey-and-team an overflowing, frilly-decorated, and plastic covered huge bowl of fresh fruit "in appreciation for the game".

Joey was greatly impressed by the gift and magnanimously announced the bowl would reside in the Deck Mess tonight and in the Engine Mess tomorrow. And then added to giggles from the Americans; "Can't wait to get at one of those apples. Thanks again, Giants!" Joey was totally relaxed…the game had been a huge success and he had at least four days or so before he had to organize Game Two!

Watching the game was the sporting goods store proprietor who elbowed his way to Joey's side to tell him; "Good basubar game, Joeee. Good news… Beeg shoes for Americans, I order today. Be day o'so befo' get here to Onomichi from Hiroshima. Fo' shu you gonna hab dem befo' nex' game!" Joey thanked the man, shook his hand and said he'd be leaving the field now to return to the ship…, and had started to do that when he saw Kozuko Minuri, his geisha friend from the Sakura Bar, in the crowd ahead of him. She was alone, with her hair "let down" and dressed in every-day, Western, housewife looking clothes. "Very attractive…and probably much more comfortable than she was in that geisha outfit!" thought Joey as he waved for her to come to him; which she did.

Upon arriving in front of him, with a huge smile, Kozuko imitated him with a loud rendition of his; **"SWEENG BATTAAH".** Joey laughed out loud. Heads turned in her direction at her shout, but all were wearing smiles. She was alone and after giving her a hug, Joey asked if she'd like to accompany him to a local seaside restaurant for some *yaki-soba*, or such, to eat. He rubbed his belly letting her know he was hungry…and then said; *"Tempura joto desu!"* or, in English; "Tempura would be very good to eat!" She smiled and took his arm.

To the Japanese that were looking on, this socializing between the two of them was also "a good thing"… as they again, smiled knowingly.

Joey felt as though, by virtue of the game, he was now accepted by a good percentage of the local population…and that relaxed him even further. After depositing his ball gear into the Toyopet 3-wheeler "truck", he took Kozuko by the arm and swung her toward the waterfront and a restaurant there.

It is to his credit that before Joey left, Slim let Joey know he'd make certain that all the B-ball gear got back to where it was supposed to go. He then told Joey to have some fun. Joey thanked Slim and left the ball field with Kozuko on his arm.

CHAPTER TWENTY FOUR

THE CHERRY BLOSSOM PARTY

Joey had only one day to enjoy the attention that was bestowed on him by the Japanese for his part in getting the ball game played. This attention consisted mainly of relatively loud **"SWEEENG BATTAH"** calls from passing locals. Joey routinely turned and waved to whoever made the call…and he thought the notoriety was fun! But "his world" was changed by the (unexpected) announcement by the Chief Engineer on Sunday, that the *entire* main engine was to be overhauled and that; "…the overhaul would start now!" This departure, from the originally planned "segmented and selective overhaul" (based upon where the engine took the most in bearing-wear) taking place over a one month period… sidelined the here-to-for, relatively relaxed atmosphere enjoyed by the ship's engineering complement.

This particular day, being a Sunday, "holiday routine" or doing *only "standing watches work"* was pursued on the ship. Still, the announcement to expand the (overhaul) work package and modify the planned timing of the expanded work-package, had immediate and adverse impact on the liberty planning by the "Black Gang". In light of this news, Joey decided that as soon as his afternoon watch was completed he would go ashore to see Kozuko and discuss "their near term planning".

This time, going to see her, he felt some urgency, so instead of walking, he took a Toyopet Taxi up the hill to the Sakura Bar. Sunday or not, there was a lot of activity up on the hill, primarily in and around the "orchard" of Cherry trees. He lost his mental focus on that activity upon her appearance at the door of the "house". As before at the ball field, her non-geisha dress followed "Western fashion" dictates. She now looked superb in her flower-patterned dress, opened at the neck white blouse, and "let down" hair… and he so advised her! She appreciated his complement with a demure *arrigato* (thanks) and invited him in for a drink… and to talk.

Upon hearing the news about his involvement in the upcoming engine overhaul, she was concerned and showed that concern in her manner when she told him about the upcoming and all consuming "Cherry Blossom" celebration. He was "tuned in" to her explanation that, as it normally was, April's "Spring Cherry Blossom Celebration" was to be the highlight of the year for Onomichi. And, in all its glory, the event was due to start in about a week. It seems that a horde of folks were expected to land in Onomichi to attend this event. They would be coming primarily from the metropolis to the West, Hiroshima, and also from Okayama to the East.

Regarding this onslaught of visitors, Kozuko noted as an aside, that she (her "geisha business") would be impacted directly, by being employed to host the visitors. It was important therefore, that the two of them plan on being together as much as possible prior to the holiday, and to finish this aspect of the planning as soon as possible.

He was not upset by the factual news she passed to him regarding her status with the visitors. He knew; *she was a geisha* and by definition, in the "entertainment business". Even with her designated as an exception, it was still somewhat difficult for him *to understand there would be any adverse impact* of having "visitors" to a spot on Honshu that earned its living primarily from visitors. This insight showed that Joey fully *understood "the bottom line" in their conversation, and that was: this upcoming holiday was very important to all in Onomichi.*

His major input to their planning was that the engine overhaul would overlap a portion of the holiday… and that he had to participate in that overhaul. He also told her that, to add to his liberty time, "getting a standby or two" for his daytime (noon to 4 PM) watch was not easy, but was possible. The major impact of that latter action was that "standbys", per se, had to paid back …and those paybacks, coupled with his regular watch, might result in him being tied to the ship for a couple of days at a time.

All told, he summed the upcoming situation up with a wave of his arm and a squinting, facially unsmiling expression. In English, he said with personal resolve; "Let's just not worry about anything at this stage of the game. I'm sure we'll be able to work out any problems as they pop up."

Resulting from their attempting to realize the most in liberty- time, the overhaul was tough on Joey and Slim. That overhaul-effort, mainly consisting for them, the repetitive handling of extremely heavy engine components, to facilitate obtaining proper bearing clearances. This was "weight lifting" kinds of work and it seriously depleted any energy reserves the two seamen might've had. Those black gang members involved with the overhaul found that they were, in the main, limited in free time to little more than eating their meals and sleeping!

Since thoughts of going on liberty were seldom in coming, Joey had the word passed to Kozuko via the sporting goods store owner, that he wouldn't be seeing her for a few days,… at least until he got used to *working the eight-hour-day* needed for the engine overhaul.

Three days into the engine overhaul, Joey got word from Kozuko that the Town was; "…going into final preparations for the annual April, "Cherry Blossum (Sakura) Festival". Further, that while the festival wouldn't be starting for another couple of days, Joey should plan on attending it as soon as possible. And it would also be most desirable if Joey could devote a few days to being "part of the working team" that was erecting and stocking the tents for the holiday up on the hill. He almost didn't know why he thought of it, but Joey's immediate thought was that the festival would cut into the time needed to field the ship's ball team for another game. As a matter of fact, the engine overhaul would also contribute to making time for the game extremely difficult.

The following day, Wednesday, starting about 1: 30 PM, Joey, bringing Slim along, made it up to where the Sakura bar proprietor was heavily engaged in raising a huge tent to house its business during the festival. Upon arrival, he and Slim went to work immediately hauling-on the tent sides to tighten the roof-canvas and in driving the spikes devoted to keeping the tent upright and taught.

The proprietor immediately came forth with the *"arrigato's (thank you's)* for this voluntary effort on the part of the two seamen. Almost, as in payment, he offered them some Kirin beer from a case he had brought to the tent from the Sakura Bar. Joey really was not a "beer drinker" so his refusal of a beer was almost expected by the proprietor. Slim, on the other hand, loved drinking beer… so, with the proprietor's help in opening the bottle, he happily accepted and drank a bottle of Kirin. The tent was subsequently erected with few problems. The follow-on project for the two seamen had the two of them carrying large hibachis from the bar to the tent.

Joey observed again that the ceramic hibachis were quite heavy! The carrying and placement of the hibachis was hard work! Also carried to the tent by the two seamen, was a small, "portable" refrigerator. The "fridge" was representative of the "leaving the heavy work for the Americans" mentality that reigned at the Sakura bar portion of the hill. In all, for that day, the two seamen remained more than just gainfully employed in the shift of the Town to the Cherry tree orchard. To underscore their fatigue, to the already tired Joey and Slim, *it seemed the carrying of items from the permanent House and Bar to the hill was never-ending!*

The overfilled "work schedule" for Joey and Slim *kept the two seamen over-tired!* Joey had "the word" put-out that the ball game that was planned to be held on Saturday, was *cancelled due to ship's business* (the engine overhaul). The crew generally took this notice in a particularly upsetting manner. They had enjoyed the game held the previous Saturday and were looking forward to this week's game. While they didn't apprise Joey of their ire, they did take issue with the "apparently unnecessary urgency" with which the engine overhaul was to be undertaken.

No matter, the engine overhaul was not to be denied. In addition to its impact on the ball-game and on Joey's liberty planning, where it really impacted Joey was in his relationship with Kozuko. Joey had taken a real liking to Kozuko, to where one might say he was overly infatuated. For Joey, "something had to give"! Since the ship had priority, Joey decided; "that something" would be his availability to enjoy her company.

They still had not had any sex or much social interaction of any sort…and with the schedules they both were following, the prospect of overcoming that problem in the immediate future, was dim. This bothered Joey. He was also a bit surprised that the "having sex issue" had taken a back seat to all else in their relationship. "It was not like him!" he thought.

CHAPTER TWENTY FIVE

GETTING TO KNOW HER

The days devoted to the combined ship and Town work-effort passed and with this "passing", Joey and Slim stopped working on both the overhaul and the Sakura Bar & Geisha House relocation. For Joey, this completion of extra work in Town was welcomed with visible relief. He thought he could now take his non-overhaul time to just enjoy his time with Kozuko, and if he played his cards correctly, also allow him to look forward to participating in the upcoming Sakura holiday. He passed the word to Kozuko again by phone, via the sporting goods store owner, that he really wanted to see and be with her for an evening...soon!

The word came back amazingly fast that Kozuko shared his desire and asked"; would he be available this evening?" It was only about 4: 30PM and he was ready to be with her right then! He told the proprietor to tell her that he was *on his way to pick her up, now* ...by taxi.

She was outside the bar when he arrived. After insuring the taxi driver would not depart, Joey stepped out of the cab and hugged her tightly. Smiling, she looked him over closely and with her fingers, touched his face immediately below his eyes. She gestured to him she thought he looked fatigued. He nodded in agreement with her observation and then gestured for her to "… forget it" and climb into the cab, and for them to leave the House. Gesturing for him to wait a moment, she climbed back into the House and returned with two smallish towels and a bar of soap.

Steering Joey back into the cab, she told the driver to take them to a close-by *sento* (communal bath house). The driver immediately understood her and with a loud "Hai!" (Yes!) he pivoted the cab back down the hill!

They arrived at the bath house in what seemed seconds. She had the small change they needed for entry and they headed for the "preparation area" where they would leave their clothes. They both disrobed and, for some reason, Joey tried to avert his gaze when she became naked. Joey found this "being naked in public" custom to be a bit unsettling. In this "preparation area" there were wooden stools for them to sit upon when cleaning themselves, and wooden buckets to hold the wash water. Joey thought; "Someone here has really done some planning. Why? In this area there was a small pool of clean hot water (o'funa ot'sui!) for their use in soaping up and rinsing off prior to entering the large (onsen furo) the hot-spring fed, public bath." They entered, but were not alone in the large bath area…and again Joey was slightly unnerved by his (now clean) nakedness. Kozuko motioned for Joey to close his eyes and just relax. He did this. It was about a half hour before they left the Bath.

Their bath behind them, Joey found he was again ensconced in another three-wheeler taxi. This time he and Kozuko were enroute to an "A-stickered" restaurant in the lower, waterfront portion of Town. He was hungry and upon entering the restaurant, persuaded Kozuko, that when she ordered his food, to order using the rotary, visual menu-models for choices. If she did this, she would not need to translate their food selections to Joey. She would just point to the dishes they were to get.

The proprietor welcomed Kozuko and Joey with; Komban-wa Kozuko San (Good evening, Miss Kozuko) and then had a very short, socially oriented conversation with her in Japanese. He led them into a small, intimate dining space with a large, lit charcoal-fired hibachi in its center. With a large smile and sweep of his arm he offered the space to the couple. Kozuko told him; "Joto desu!" (This is good!) The proprietor immediately turned to Joey and rather loudly exclaimed; "SWEENG BATTUUUR!" Now giggling, he left the dining space with the comment in Japanese for both guests; *"Irasche immassen."* (Loosely translated; "Welcome to my humble place.")

For Joey, the dinner started with a Kobe beefsteak grilled by Kozuko, followed by a (soba) noodle- filled broth and finished with a large dish of cut-up, fresh fruit for dessert. Warm *"Ichiban"* ("Number 1" graded) saki arrived at their table in a beautifully decorated small decanter with matching cups. The saki was served by Kozuko, and indeed, she hovered over his entire meal as she would have at the geisha house. Her offerings of food to him were accompanied by "musically sounding" Japanese phrases, one of which referred to him by name…, a phrase he did not understand, but appreciated.

The proprietor approached their table at the conclusion of their meal and exclaimed to Joey; "Kore-wa Nihon riyori desu. Meshiara-gareru (Joey San) desho na." (This is our (Japanese) food. I hope you like it, Joey San.) Joey thought Kozuko did an exceptionally good job of translating this mammoth chunk of conversational Japanese to Joey, and in response, his belly rub with a "big smile" carried his praise of the food to the owner. The owner then requested of Kozuko that she play the *samisen*, a guitar-like instrument, for Joey and the rest of his customers. Kozuko agreed to play.

The owner became ecstatic when she agreed to play. Joey did not know it but, as a geisha, playing the samisen was an entertainment ability that she had had to acquire "early in the becoming-a-geisha game". She played beautifully and sung along with the music! She was a fine entertainer. Joey was very proud of her!

After some fifteen minutes of her playing, Joey and Kozuko "squared-up" with the owner on the bill. The owner made a point of letting Joey know that the saki was not on the bill but had been provided as a gift. With several "Dozo's" ("Please allow me…") he let Joey and Kozuko know that he was proud to pay for their drinks. With a slight bow and the words; "Arrigato gozai-imasu!", Kozuko accepted the owner's gift for both of them.

It was now getting a bit late in the evening so Kozuko suggested they go to a local, but very nice, also "A-stickered", waterfront tourist hotel, the Onomichi Oteru. Kozuko's rationale; There, they could sit in the bar for a drink or two prior to bedtime. Joey agreed but also advised Kozuko that he had to be back aboard the ship for his Midnight to 4

AM Watch. She nodded her understanding. Joey was amazed at how Kozuko picked up the nuances of his spoken and gestured English. She had no problems with his plans. Joey found he was becoming very "fond" of her. "Perhaps *fond* isn't a strong enough word to describe how I feel about her." He thought.

Knowing it would be the better part of a month before the MC GOWAN's bottom plating would be repaired, Joey asked how long the Sakura celebration would continue. Kozuko noted that the Cherry blossoms themselves would be at the top of their blooming period for only the next week and a half, more or less, but the visiting population from Hiroshima would be underfoot for at least the next two weeks. Joey reacted by letting Kozuko know that *he planned to be part of her celebration and life…*and then later… *for as long as he (and the ship) stayed in Onomichi.*

Holding hands they walked across the street to the small hotel. Joey was feeling very "up" and in the middle of the street did an amazingly graceful imitation of dance steps he'd seen Fred Astaire do in a movie with Ginger Rogers. Kozuko was also "up" for some fun and smilingly, gave Joey another loud "SWEENG BATTAH" as he spun her around in the "dance"!

Shoes left at the door, they smilingly entered the hotel and Kozuko bartered with the proprietor over the room rate. Her arguments were convincing since the hotel man didn't do much smiling after giving the pair the welcome, verbal standard; *"Irashe Imassen".* Joey gave the man *the decided upon* 1,000 Y room rent, and at that point, the proprietor led the way to their room carrying two steaming-hot face towels. He had to make another two trips to their room; one for a pitcher of cold drinking water with tray and two glasses, and the second to deliver a pan of hot coals to seed their hibachi.

Kozuko had seated Joey on the straw mat next to the hibachi while she determined from the hotel man, the location of the bedding they would use. Prior to dismissing the hotel man she insured he would make a call on the room at 11 PM to awaken Joey, so he'd be able to return to the ship in time for his watch. Joey was impressed! *She left nothing to chance.*

It took Joey almost no time to start disrobing while Kozuko attended to the hibachi and "making the bed". He really was infatuated with her and thought it somewhat amusing that in contrast with his earlier port stops, this one in Onomichi did not have him looking for just *any lady* to have sex with, as his first priority. *He just wanted her company! Further, he thought, considering all that had transpired between them prior to their being in this room, this relationship could almost be compared to their being a married couple.* He welcomed this thought.

He held the bed-sheet aloft between them to insure her privacy upon undressing. Her softly whispered *arrigato* (thank you) showed her appreciation for his consideration. They then kissed and caressed each other in preparation for sex… and while dropping to the mattress. He thought again of how much she had "grown upon him" between the time they had met at the Sakura Bar and now, together in this hotel. Their love making was emotionally soft and physically tender, and completely satisfying to both. Upon its completion and while having a Camel, his thoughts drifted to Betty in Beaumont and his realization that *Betty couldn't hold a candle to Kozuko in any category.*

They lay talking until he had to dress for his return to the ship. After he dressed, he hugged her, told her he was going to call her "Koz", for short…and then told her he was falling in love with her. He didn't know for certain whether he should refer to her Japanese boyfriend at this somewhat sensitive time, but he did anyway. His comment was; *"Aijin anata wa o-ie* (your boyfriend or not), *Akio*, had seen you for his last time!" Her return comment was a simple; *"Hai!"* ("Yes!") Joey kissed her again with deep emotion and then left the hotel and her, for the ship.

His mind was active during his return to the dock and ship. He knew he should have asked for her personal telephone number, if she had one, and where and when specifically they should again meet,… at least until she moved up the hill for the Sakura celebration. He was a bit upset with himself for these oversights until he saw Akio, dressed in his working clothes, walking in the shadows behind him. Not wanting to stir the situation up to a fighting point if he could help it, he acknowledged the "boyfriend's" presence with a slightly loud and directed at Akio *"Kum ban' wa!"* (Good evening!). Joey received a "waive off" from Akio in return. Akio did not move past Joey, so Joey turned and continued on his way to the dock with Akio trailing.

Upon reaching the ship's main deck level, Joey saw that Big Tom was watching him from the ship, and actually was in position to have seen Joey from the time he entered the dry dock. When they were almost face to face, Tom took the lead and related to Joey that he, Joey "…had been followed into the dock by a Japanese dock worker" …who had "kept his eyes on you, Joey, for almost the entire time that you took to get aboard the ship." Joey came back with; "Thanks for keeping an eye on me this late in the evening, but I knew that that Dude was behind me. He was the local boyfriend of a Japanese lady I'm taking up with…and *it's serious between me an' her!* He's gonna have to put on a pair of sneakers if he's thinking of jumping me. I know he's there an' I think I can handle him if it comes to that."

Tom's come back was simply; "OK. But keep your eyes and ears open! This joint is his playground…not yours! And, would you believe it? I'm getting used to having you around. Hate to have to break in another lubber at this stage of the voyage, if'n you get hurt. By the way, I've seen that "ex-boyfriend" enough recently, that I can recognize him in a crowd. I'll keep an eye on him…" Joey thanked Tom again and let him know that he'd relieve him of the watch duties after he changed clothes. Then, Joey finally asked; "Slim get back aboard? Kinda lost track of him recently." Tom just nodded "Yes". "Gonna look him up prior to watch. Gotta talk some stuff over with him." Joey said while he turned toward the mid-ship's house entrance and the Engineering Berthing spaces. See you soon to relieve you, Tom."

Upon his entry into the berthing space Joey saw Slim at the desk with pen and paper, head down in composing something. Joey opened with; "Hi Slim. Getting a note off to the wife?" Slim nodded and waved to Joey but in so doing, didn't break his attention to his letter. Joey added; "Want to talk to you. Have an idea it might be in my best interest to move ashore while we're here in Onomichi. …Like to know what you think about that idea. Seems me and Kozuko are "a thing" now. I really dig that chick! Don't want her to be splitting her time between me and being an employed geisha. With the upcoming Sakura Festival that'll run for maybe a couple of weeks, think I've got to move out on this "moving out" thing…and get and stay together with her real soon!"

Slim had put his pen down and payed Joey his full attention when Joey hit the "…moving ashore…" part. "Y'all shore that'd be 'ow yer a'thinkin? Big move fo' a ship-driver inna middle of a trip. Ah'm not a'gonna get inta wha' happens t'yo' gal when we hoist anchor for the States…but it shore as hell is somethin' yo' have to think about! Fer example, y'all gonna marry her a'fore we leave?"

With the last comment, Joey raised his hand to cut Slim off. "Hey, you gotta know that I haven't gotten these thoughts across to Kozuko as yet…but that marriage thing doesn't sound so bad. Wanted to try all this stuff out on you first. Y'also ought to know that I've been toying with the thought of bringing her back to the States with me when I pay off this Liberty. All that said, *y'gotta know I'm really not gonna "jump ship" over being with her."* Slim now raised his arm, palm toward Joey, and shook his head almost in disbelief at what he was hearing.

"Listen Joey. You're fully grown and can do some deep thinkin'. But ah'll be damned… dis idea of your'n kinda takes the nut-cake….at least while you're here aboard dis ship. S'pose y'all really do what you're a-sayin' about livin' ashore. How 'bout items lak showin' up fer ship emergencies er other all-hands-calls, or routine items lak getting' your meals 'er bein' called fer watch…an' more? All ah kin finally think of is; livin' ashore 'tween watches and day work 'll need yer Engineer's OK too…an' ah think he's gonna flip out when y'all ask him!"

Joey thanked Slim for "leveling" with him. He mentioned that he thought it was a great idea to talk over with Slim the whole "Kozuko-related-issue". He added for emphasis; "Just know that *I'm not in the doing something stupid* thing right now! I just fell in love with that chick!"

CHAPTER TWENTY SIX

"SAKURA" TIME

Upon awakening from a very short, post-Watch- sleep-session, Joey dressed for and then had his ship- board breakfast. Earlier, he had given up on the idea to immediately extract Kozuko from the Geisha House and put her into an apartment …but he did not set aside his concern that the upcoming Sakura holiday might cause both of them real anguish. Why? To Joey, the thought of being kept apart for an extended period was intolerable …so he rethought the problem. He decided finally that "Having an apartment was really the way to go to avoid some of these *sure-to-come* problems that would affect their relationship!"

Slim followed Joey into the Engine Mess and took his normal place at their table. He wasted no time in obtaining a cup of coffee and letting Otis know to order his "routine breakfast". He then faced Joey and let him know that he, Slim, had rethought their conversation of the previous night and now actually thought that setting Kozuko up in an apartment might be the best way for Joey to go.

Joey was not evasive in responding to Slim. "I've already made up my mind to do just that! By the way, was talking with Otis just before sitting down to eat, and he told me that he got it from the 8 to 12 Watch, that we'll be putting the finishing touches on the engine overhaul today… and might be even able to "jack the engine over" early this afternoon. Regarding my planning, I think that'll be just perfect!"

Following breakfast he told Slim he'd be going ashore and would check on Koz and if possible, "… get her into an apartment". This plan of action again seemed the perfect way to go…and the cost of renting an apartment, even at the inflated market price because of the upcoming Sakura event, was deemed to be well worth it!

Immediately upon going ashore, Joey rented an apartment from the sporting goods store proprietor and it was located just above the store. That particular apartment really was most beneficial for Joey since it was close enough that; "…he could almost stumble out of the dry dock and into the apartment…and vice versa". Kozuko moved in the same afternoon Joey obtained the space. Unknown to Joey, Kozuko had even made arrangements that day to buy her way out of the geisha house entirely, and had used part of her savings to close that deal.

Back aboard the ship, Joey again "plastered the bulletin boards" in all the messes with his announcement of the second baseball game to be held, as was the first one, at 10 AM the upcoming Saturday. He left word with his new landlord, the store owner, to; "…please handle the details for the game with Yoshio, the baseball coordinator".

The crew took no time at all to heap thanks upon Joey for setting up the second ball game. Almost to a man, they looked forward to the game! Joey, himself, was pleased to be able to get the game scheduled this close to the time of the Sakura celebration, and this promised to be the last opportunity for a game prior to the ship coming out of the dry dock… and departing Onomichi. Kozuko was very pleased that Joey had found the time to do this baseball planning. She had become very proud of him and his acceptance by the local population… and knew that the game would add to that acceptance.

For the apartment, the first items on Kozuko's shopping list were a tatami (mat) to sleep upon, an hibachi to cook upon and the food needed to serve Joey his first supper, and then breakfast… in their new digs. Joey himself had packed his handbag for the first stay in the apartment with two changes of under wear and socks and a change of liberty-going clothes.

Further, in the back of his mind, he was glad he had "paid his dues" in helping to set up the Sakura tent and related where-with-all on the hill. Now, nobody would trouble him for any further participation on "hill projects". Also, now he and Kozuko would be *accepted vacationing guests* at the celebration; instead of just being participants in setting-up the holiday area.

Kozuko insured Joey understood that the "small town", Onomichi's, preparation for the "party" was almost the equal of the "Cherry Blossom celebration preparations" in Kamakura, one of the nation's largest. She also let him know that she planned on being a geisha during a large part of the celebration. "The tips would be enormous... and she and Joey certainly could use the extra money!" was how she put it. Joey didn't argue since he knew she would be employed as a geisha in the same tent he helped erect, and he planned on being there at the tent as often as his work on the ship permitted.

With the completion of shipboard work associated with the engine overhaul, his (now rested) outlook on virtually everything improved immensely. He found he was actually looking forward to the Saturday ball game and to making daily trips to Koz at the apartment. Both these issues seemed to be totally "under control" and his disposition improved accordingly. Additionally, with each of his thoughts associated with Koz, he mentally reaffirmed his "love for her"! Underlying this "love" was that Koz bestowed her total attention on him whenever they were together.

While this effort on her part would seem to be "expected", to Joey it was a very welcome change to what he had previously experienced from the ladies in his life. He just couldn't believe it, but...excepting the women he met on this Liberty trip, from Ellie Massimino in Brooklyn, who stopped at almost nothing in her attempts to keep him from going to sea,... through the callous, monetary outlook and demands of the prostitute, Betty, in Beaumont. *Those ladies expected him to alter his life to meet their desires.* **Koz didn't!** Further, he honestly loved her and thought repetitively that he should marry her and bring her back to the States. He also thought *that he couldn't do better in selecting a mate than by selecting her.*

It was early April and it was very early Thursday morning when Joey dropped in to see his "landlord" and request he contact Yoshio to arrange for baseball equipment to use for practice by the crew-ballplayers that afternoon. He was a bit late in showing up at the mess for breakfast but Otis saw that he was hungry and arranged for a full breakfast to be served to him. Jokingly, Joey allowed as how because of this special treatment he was getting, he'd insure he saved the pitching slot for Otis this Saturday. Joking back, Otis said that would be fine... providing Joey promised to catch all the curve balls thrown to him.

Toast, over-medium eggs, crisp bacon and home fries behind him, Joey double-checked the baseball sign-up sheets to insure he had at least ten ball players signed up for Saturday. He had twelve signed up. As the time approached 7: 00 AM he shifted into clean but heavily oil-stained, working duds. It was April and enough into modest, Spring-like weather that he chose light chinos for the upcoming engine room work.

The Second Assistant gave Joey a particularly warm welcome at the muster for the morning's work...and assigned Joey to working with him on repacking throttle valves for the auxiliary machinery in the engine room. Slim gave Joey a quick smile and thumbs-up at this work assignment. Joey well-recalled that Slim had previously mentioned that to him, the Second was concentrating upon preparing Joey to sit for his Third Assistant (Steam) Engineer's examination, and this thumbs-up probably referred to that issue. Joey then put those thoughts out of his mind and went to arm himself with the tools and materials he'd need for this work.

The work went well. The Second relied on Joey to properly cut the strips of packing to go around the valve stems, to properly "take-up" on the valve packing glands, and finally, to properly lubricate the valve packing glands and valve stems receiving this maintenance. When they broke for "coffee time" at 10 AM, the second accompanied Joey to the Black Gang Mess to draw his coffee there. Enroute, he let Joey know he knew of Joey's renting the apartment "on the beach" and also let Joey know he really didn't want Joey "...to be living off the ship". Joey was surprised that the Second knew of the result of *his very recent escapades* with Koz and was also a bit upset that the Second was getting into his personal life.

Joey responded with; "You've gotta know this, Second, and that's that I'm not thinking of living off the ship. I'm just trying to set my girl up for living independently outside the geisha house, in an apartment. I'm serious about this lady and want nothing but the best for her. …You know? You've been a real friend to me and I'd like to introduce you to her. Maybe we can have a dinner together sometime soon; …maybe after the game Saturday." With a huge smile, the Second came back with; "You've got it. It's a date."

Following day-work knock-off at noon Joey shifted into his ball-playing clothes and shoes and, with Slim, made for the cab-stand and to the ball park for practice. Joey was tickled when he saw Koz in the stands bordering the third base line. He again thought she was the best thing that had happened to him in a long time. Recalling the outstanding post game "dinner date" he had with the Second, Joey eased up to Koz and let her know of this promise. *She immediate broke out in a huge smile and excitedly told him she would be the cook …and that they would have the dinner at about 6 PM and at their* apartment. Joey went back to the dugout also wreathed in a big smile, thinking again that *he really did love this woman! She thinks of everything!*

The weather had been holding with no rain falling for the past several days, so the field was "fast" and the practice had little dirtying-affect on their clothes,… so no uniform washing was in the cards prior to the game. To Joey this was a very effective practice… and included Tex throwing for batting practice and then "hitting fungo" for infield defensive work. Joey thought that for such an inauspicious start between him and Tex, the "Deckape" was becoming indispensable to the ball team.

Not being able to keep from thinking of her, Joey was profoundly happy with Koz being readily accepted by the crew. He left the dugout and hugged her. Tex, who observed the show of affection, loudly inquired; "Hey leader…You gonna have a pre-game-practice, or what? We're running out of afternoon here!" The rest of the practice went beautifully!

On Saturday, the weather was perfect for the game. It was a glorious, Spring day and there wasn't a cloud in the sky to spoil the unabbating sunshine that blanketed the field. The seven inning ball game went quite like their first game, with the MC GOWAN crew losing again... and again, by one run. Joey continued with his **SWING BATTER** chatter from behind the plate and the local kids in the stands again echoed this chatter with each Japanese batter. Otis had three more strikeouts in the second game than he had in the first and Joey observed that if they were to play again, the Messman would turn into an Onomichi "fixture" because of that baseball pitching prowess.

The game ended in the mid-afternoon and after the post-game fruit basket exchanging ceremony, Joey went to what was rapidly becoming his favorite watering hole, the A-stickered waterfront restaurant (and bar). He was accompanied to the bar by Slim and a couple of other celebrating seamen from the team. Their conversation and laughter were loud enough, when walking to the bar, to turn "local" heads. Joey thought the celebrating, per se, was a little "over the top" since the ship's team *lost the game.*

Big Tex came along with them after personally insuring the borrowed baseball equipment were on their way back to the Japanese team. Joey thanked him for that bit of caring and offered to buy him his first beer. In turn, Tex thanked Joey for the beer after he loudly expressed his appreciation for the ball games that "...you (Joey) organized".

Shortly after the first beer was consumed, the Second Assistant Engineer made his appearance at the bar. He immediately came up to Joey who had been small-talking with Slim and Tex, and started his end of the conversation with; "Hey, heard this game was as good as the first one... sorry I missed it. But, sure don't want to miss the Kozuko-prepared dinner, so I'm here early for that bit!" Joey smilingly told the Second that Koz was off preparing that dinner, as they spoke. Listening at Joey's elbow, Big Tom chimed in with; "Hey, if'n that gal fixes enough chow, can I come too?" There were giggles all around.

The second Kirin beer went down as easily as the first had, and Joey offered to the Second that they both ought to save some yen (money) and shift their drinking locale to Joey and Koz's apartment. There was no argument to the suggestion and the two seamen left the bar for the short walk to the (above the sporting goods store) apartment.

Dinner was served by Koz starting at 6 PM. She had built the bill of fare around shrimp tempura, soba (a fish and noodle soup) and pork-fried rice. Shortly after they arrived, the very best saki that money could buy was being warmed over the hibachi, …and, when warm enough, Koz served it to both Joey and the Second along with an appetizer of thinly sliced, soy sauce impregnated, char-broiled strips of beef steak. Both men thanked her warmly for the delicious appetizer and, in geisha-fashion, Koz just bowed demurely to their graciousness.

She started the pre-dinner conversation with the traditional Japanese dining room welcome; "Kore-wa Nihon ryori desu. Meshiagareru', …desho ne." (This is Japanese food. I hope you like it.) After serving the soup and tasting it, she tapped her head and added; "Kono'-suimono-wa oishii' desu. Ne?" (I think this soup is delicious… Do you agree?) Joey translated Koz's conversational Japanese to the Second, who responded with nods. Joey surprised himself with his progress in "the language". In short, not only was the appetizer and soup superb, but *the entire meal was an unqualified success*!

It was at the time of the post-dinner sweet role that the Second leaned over to Joey and whispered; "Hey I've become a real fan of Kozuko… and of your relationship with her. I know you didn't ask for my opinion, but I think you'd be doing well if it ever came to you and the lady getting married, or something. I'd like you to know that I agree with you in your general planning to "…bring her back to the States" with you. She's a winner! Tell you what; when we're down to the last day or two in the graving dock, I'll push the Hitachi Iron Works people for use of their trans-Pacific phone line to the States… for you to get in touch with your folks regarding getting someone who'll be there at the airport to meet her (Pan Am) Clipper when it arrives on the West Coast. You know, she should be met by someone who'll guide her through the beaurocracy she'll face upon entry into the USA. Also, I'll make sure you get to our Consulate in Hiroshima to get the full "skinny" on what it takes from your end to make all this planning work."

Joey listened to the Second's every word. Having the man "in his corner" as relating to Koz's upcoming trip in his, Joey's, behalf meant a lot to him. He could now finalize and solve the alluded to; *many beaurocratic stumbling blocks* that stood in his way, both here in Japan and in the USA, to get her to his family Stateside. He wasted no time in capitalizing on the Second's offer. He proposed; "How about early Monday morning we get going to Hiroshima and start the marriage process at the Consulate? I think that once that marriage hurdle is surmounted, getting Koz a Visa is gonna get a lot easier. Also, if the timing allows, maybe we can get her a plane ticket that'll get her to the West Coast." The Second nodded his concurrence. Joey continued; "You know? All of a sudden, I'm excited about getting this Visa and travel stuff resolved. I don't know what, if any, administrative delays are built into the process, but our getting started early is certain to help."

After the meal and the extensive conversation that followed it, Joey and Koz both walked the departing Second to the door. It was still a beautifully clear and warm day, even if the hour was late and darkness enveloped the Town. The Second while in the doorway let his glance wander up the hill to the Cherry Tree acreage and its illumination. "Boy, they're getting ready for a real shindig. Never did see that much lighting in use for an outdoor event. Just might go on up and participate in the festivities. It'd be fun!"

Joey immediately responded to the Second's comment with; "Koz and I are gonna hit her "house on the hill" and just might do a bit of celebrating of our own for our upcoming wedding. I like that "Onomichi shovel song"; …and the dance that the locals do to it. Our "House" has that music on a disc and the ground is hard enough to be danced on!"

The Second left within minutes and did not go up the hill, or take a cab anywhere. He immediately turned for the entrance to the graving dock and the SS MC GOVERN therein. Joey swung into the apartment holding Koz by the forearm and headed for the small pile of dirty dishes.

Dishes done in the sink, the two put on light sweaters and took a cab up to the Sakura Festival layout. Joey gave Koz a hug while in the cab and told her in English; "Thanks for the perfect dinner and evening. I think the Second had a ball! I know I did… and was very proud of you at the same time. You put on the perfect dinner… and that was the first time any girl did that for me.' Koz immediately came back in heavily accented English with; "I proud of you too with base-a baur (baseball) you do. Today game *ichiban* (number one)! Aur (all) in Onomichi know you an' (that makes) me proud! *Takusan (a lot of) proud!*

After some last minute directions to the cabby, they pulled in right in front of the Sakura Bar & Geisha House. The proprietor was tickled to see them and blurted out two *Irashe' immassen* (s). "Welcome to my place of business"; and then reached for the Tori Whiskey bottle. Koz immediately got the man into a conversation having to do with how his business was faring. The response brought out a warm smile from Kozuko and she gave him a hug. Drink in hand, Joey asked to have the Onomichi- shovel-dance record played. And from a drawer in the desk under the cash register another of the geishas pulled the appropriate record.

Joey wasted no time in holding out his right hand for Koz to take in preparation for their dance. She declined and directed, by repeating; *Annata wa*'! "You (do the dancing!" The other geisha, seeing the confused look on Joey's face, went into a slight crouch facing Joey and with her hands raised to chest height, started to do the "shovel dance" in time with the music. Now dancing, Joey chimed in with what he remembered of the words to the tune.

His memory consisted of almost one stanza"
Onomichi minato' wa
Ano hito' yo
Canzashi a-toma
Dum da de'ed um da da
Loosely translated by Koz, the message carried by the tune was;
Oh you Onomichi Harborites
Listen all you people
When at this affair
Come to a stop (with your everyday) "watery affairs"
And join in the party.
(and so on… with a double count to the tune)
The dancing geisha hardly moved her feet as she "doubled the shovel motion" in each direction, and in time with the beat, but she was dancing happily… and dancing well! Joey, watching closely, joined the

geisha in the latter part of the dance and to the surprise of all, did quite well. Joey thought the record ended too soon. He enjoyed the dance.

The party carried on into the night and when the time hit 11 PM and Joey was on his third drink, Koz turned him toward the door and jokingly waived him to go outside. It was time for Joey to return to the ship. He was supposed to relieve Big Tom at midnight. Joey asked for a cab to take him back down the hill and to the graving dock. The proprietor reached under the cash register for the phone and did what Koz told him to do.

The cab took Joey to the entrance for the graving dock. Joey, stepping outside the cab, noted the weather was still perfect so he lit a Camel and squatted on the curb to enjoy the ambience of it all. Cigarette finished he started into the dock and saw that, "ex-boyfriend", Akio was already at work painting the ship's waterline. He was standing on a "yo-yo-pole" platform along the shop's side but was well out of Joey's path to the ship and to his mid-watch, so… Joey put him out of his mind.

CHAPTER TWENTY SEVEN

GETTING HITCHED

After shifting into working clothes Joey entered the Mess for a quick snack… and there sat Slim. Jokingly, Joey said to Slim; "We've just have to stop meeting like this… but I have something to tell you." Slim came right back with; "Anythang as nutty as your movin' off'n the ship?" Joey responded with; "Tomorrow's a week-day, Monday, and me and Koz, and maybe the Second are gonna hop a ferry to Hiroshima durin' the off-watch time. Me an' Koz are gonna get married…an' when that happens, I'd like for you to be a formal witness to the wedding. The ultimate goal is to be able to bring her back to the States so I'm going to try the Consulate Office for the forms to be submitted. Also I think I'll need signatures for that back-up paper work. Gonna try to get a hold of the forms in Hiroshima but if that don't work, will have to get them from the Embassy in Tokyo.

The next morning, Monday, came …starting at 06 30. Joey was already in his finest attire and Slim was also dressed nicely. Both had showered and shaved and plastered-down their hair. They were ready for the upcoming wedding!

In the Mess Joey got on the sound powered phone and dialed the Second's stateroom number. The Second got on the line and asked Joey to wait a moment on the call as he had information that might alter Joey's planning for the day. Joey alerted, lost his smile fearing the "worst news possible, then said; "Don't sugar coat it… just let me know what direction we're to take today. You know I want to marry Koz so maybe we ought to limit our efforts today to getting the Japanese license to do that… right here in Onomichi. Also, since we're gonna be here for a little more than a week, we should have the time to take this thing one step at a time."

The Second concurred with Joey's altered plan for the day after explaining that to get Koz to the States, Joey first had to obtain and then completely fill out the paperwork for "Fiance Immigration " for the State Department. Following that, the form review process promises to take up to a few more months prior to getting the OK on shipping Koz Stateside." Joey then said; "Hey, me and Koz are gonna hit the pavement today and get as far as we can on just getting hitched. Who knows, but I might be calling you later on to be a witness. We'll see what happens this morning. I'll be telling Slim the same thing… you wouldn't believe it but *he buffed up this morning as shiny as a new penny.* Hate to have him waste the effort so if the wedding happens and he comes along, we'll be having a big brunch… on me."

Joey and Koz knew that in the Hiroshima Prefecture (where Onomichi was located) things like the issuance of Marriage Licenses fall to the resident Township of the applicants. This in mind, Joey and Koz "took off" for the Onomichi Town (Government) Building immediately upon their finishing morning coffee at the apartment. The Licensing Office was open when they arrived, so *Koz became the spokes person for the couple.* She stated their purpose for coming there and presented an official-looking identification card and asked for the License Request Form. It was handed to her along with an instruction sheet that noted, as required in the States, the testing for blood type identification and satisfactory "Rhesus" matching… was needed prior to marriage in Japan.

The results of this test would ultimately inform all interested parties as to whether there might be a survival problem with the offspring. The laboratory results of this testing could be expected by the applicants "…within a day of submission". Since they were the day's first and only customers, the normal, beaurocracy-caused delays were set aside and the technician had the results- paperwork for the test completed within an hour.

They passed the blood type test; …and there promised to be no "blood type problem" threatening their offspring. They immediately took the lab results right back to the licensing office. Sitting at a table there, they completed the marriage application form…took it to the desk and were presented with their license. Further, since Koz was perfectly happy with a "Western Style Wedding", and not be burdened with a traditional Shinto (kimono wearing) affair, her western style clothes were perfectly adequate for the ceremony. So, all Joey and the lady had to do at this point was find a person authorized to perform the ceremony …and then for Joey, to do so.

Not having gone to any Christian church in Onomichi, Joey was reluctant to stretch his luck by surprising the local Catholic priest with an off-the-wall "…will you marry us?" request. He recalled that ship Captains were authorized to perform marriage ceremonies, so upon returning to the waterfront, Joey telephoned the Second to see if he would ask the Captain if he'd "go along" …and perform one. The Second said; "No problem, I'm just finishing lunch. So, just as soon as we hang up, I'll go ask him. By the way; where are you at?" And with the knowledge of them being at the athletic equipment store near the Graving Dock entrance and then getting the phone number for that place, he hung up saying he'd call right back with the results.

Joey and Koz were quite hungry by this time of the day, but put off going next door, to the restaurant until after they had gotten the Second's call. He did not keep them waiting long. He let them know that the Skipper thought it would be "…an honor to officiate at the ceremony". He also let them know that the Skipper had "… married people before… during the War and the Captain had said; "…by the way, I'm an ordained Baptist Minister in Texas…and that's where we departed from." And that the Skipper had the ceremony wording on a paper he carried with him just for this purpose.

Joey was beside himself with pleasure at how this wedding thing had progressed through the day to this point. Quite nervously he asked the Second if the Skipper had mentioned when he would be available to perform the task. The Second asked Joey how many folks are needed to be witnesses "…'cause the Captain is ready this afternoon…if you've got the paperwork in order." Joey responded; "Doesn't really say but, think two witnesses would do the job… and I've got the paperwork with me. Matter of fact, the ink ain't dry on it yet!"

Joey then told the Second; "… to try to set the thing up for an hour from now… or about 2: 30'ish. Koz and I still haven't gotten a thing to eat since the rice rolls this morning in the apartment, and there's a superb restaurant just 20 yards from where I'm calling from. And, I know I've been forgetting to thank you for all you've done for Koz and me… so (shouting into the phone) *Thanks a bunch!* The Second just replied; "You've got it! See you in a bit under an hour."

A very light lunch inside them, Joey and Koz eased into the Graving Dock and onto the ship. Joey took Koz into the Engineering Berthing Area to see his assigned quarters and to get to his locker where he had stowed a ring his Dad had given him. The ring was a "man's ring" and had a relative large diamond (with a large and quite visible flaw) on one half of its face, and a well-cut blue sapphire on the other half. Upon retrieving it from its hiding placebehind a metal "crease" on a support for the locker's top shelf, Joey led the way for them both to the "Skipper's Cabin", some three decks above.

Both Slim and the Second were having a smoke and some petty conversation on the weather deck's "holding platform" just outside the "Cabin". While totally unexpected by Joey, Sawada-san from the athletic equipment store was with the two Americans and was trying to get his views into the conversation…but with little success. They all forgot their conversation and sprung to being fully alert upon seeing Koz; and then went to hug her in a happy-display of "congratulations" for the upcoming wedding. Joey just beamed in appreciation and the fact that she was well thought of, and very happy! He knew that; wedding aside, their (the Americans' in the party) displays of emotion "made her day". Joey smiled with the thought that he now had three witnesses! "Let's get on with it!" he thought aloud… and knocked on the Captain's Cabin door.

The Skipper was awaiting their arrival. He had a bottle of Chevas Regal Scotch Whiskey and a half dozen glasses on a coffee table in his Waiting (Living) Room and pointed to that set-up while greeting them, saying; "For after the ceremony…". He asked Joey if he'd like to relax for a few minutes and Joey came right back with; "Nope! Let's just marry us… please".

The Captain set up a wooden lectern some three feet in from his entry door and taking his place behind it, indicated where he wanted Joey and Koz to stand …and behind them, he placed the three witnesses. He was separately advised by Joey that Sawada-san was to be the translator to insure Koz understood the wording to be pronounced to make her and Joey a married couple. The Captain then placed a "an expensive" camera on to the coffee table, "…for after the ceremony."…he explained to no one in particular. It was apparent to Joey the Captain had thought the entire process out, and Joey was appreciative of his concern.

The Captain then was provided the License and attendant paperwork for the wedding and Joey gave Slim custody of the ring his Dad had given him, and that he planned to place on Koz's wedding-finger. Joey was a bit surprised when the Skipper reached into his desk's upper drawer and brought out the ship's (unique) "SS CHARLES MC GOVERN" US Postal Station (also known as its official Notary Public) Press. Joey initially didn't realize it, but the Skipper was going to use the press to formally "raise his signature" on the wedding document. Joey also didn't know that the (Texas) Notary Public title the Captain held allowed him to perform the ceremony; since they departed that State on this trip.

The Captain then started the ceremony. The "We are gathered here in sight of the Lord to bind in matrimony this young man, Joseph Vicenzo, and this young lady Kozuko Minuri ". The ceremony continued and included the time-honored vows; "…to love, honor and obey", and… "to hold in sickness and health." With Sawada San translating for Kozuko, the ceremony took probably five minutes longer than it would have if all were conversant in English. It was noted by all participants that the "ring" portion of the affair almost took a humorous turn because the ring was obviously several sizes too large for Kozuko. The Captain softly said at that time that he was certain Joey would get it to fit using some tape… until he could get to a local jeweler to have the ring sized properly. Slim had the tape in his pocket and did the chore without problem.

Joey happily noted that Sawada San was puffed-up with pride at standing in for Koz's family. Koz gave him a kiss for his obviously difficult (but successful) translation of the Captain's words into Japanese, and when the drinks were poured following the ceremony, she insured he was handed the first glass. Upon the ceremony completion, Joey shook hands with all attendees and individually thanked them for their support and participation. Posing for the photos the Captain was taking; was another story. Joey uncomfortably concluded the Skipper was "…as bad as his (Joey's) father in taking too much time in posing the subjects for the pictures."

It took the post-wedding party another 30 minutes to "run out of steam" in celebrating. Joey again thanked the Second and the Captain for their efforts and was a touch surprised when he was advised that Big Tom, in arranging for a *"honeymoon relief"* for Joey's afternoon watch, had "covered the details" to insure the couple had the wedding-afternoon through the next morning, to themselves. The Chief Engineer concurred in "Joey …not (being) needed in the plant" for that period of time.

To the married couple; this was the best afternoon of their lives! They both wore almost "fixed smiles" when the crowd broke up prior to dinner. In retiring to the apartment they acknowledged to each other that they were absolutely fatigued by this very trying day! This was however, a very young couple… and they thought nothing of cranking into their planning for the day, a visit to the public hot bath and then a late dinner at their favorite restaurant on the waterfront of the Town.

CHAPTER TWENTY EIGHT

FAREWELL AND UNDERWAY

The wedding preceded the planned departure of the Liberty ship by a mere three days. Taking on consumables, fueling and being available for a light cargo load-out from Japan to the US of A all took place subsequent to Joey's wedding, but all events required Joey's participation in the needed, on-board efforts... to make them happen. Koz "understood his leaving" but Joey still would've "Given a month's pay..." for a longer honeymoon and for more "together time" in readying her for his departure.

He didn't have the luxury of having more time so he got on the graving dock's official telephone for a call to his mother. Letting her know that he had gotten married was for him, a difficult chore in itself. Asking for her to travel to California to meet Koz... and then to take Koz with her to Brooklyn to await Joey's return, was all something else entirely. His mother was very surprised upon getting the "news", but to her credit, she listened intently and patiently to Joey's telling of the wedding, but then, following all this news, got into the details of the "timing and plans" for actually getting Koz to the United States. Joey explained that with local Japanese "legal help", he completed the paperwork to get her a "Fiance' Visa", but the expected Consulate action on this request was predicted to take a long time to materialize. He gave Mr. Sawada's address and phone number to his mother along with the knowledge that Mr. Sawada (San) was his "legal point of contact" on the entire affair, and that he'd have Sawada San give his Mom an introductory phone call. On the financial side of the actions taken or contemplated, Joey let his Mom know that Koz was fairly self sufficient but that he would insure she had enough money for the ticket Stateside... plus some "insurance dollars" for any unexpected problems that might arise during her trip. Joey concluded with; "...the introductory call with Sawada would happen ...tomorrow; at the same time of day as this call." His Mom let Joey know that she understood his problem and would talk over the whole "plan" with Joey's father,... and would be ready for; tomorrow's phone call".

As "tomorrows" will, it came, as did his follow-up phone call with his Mom (and as needed for details, included by extensions) in the call: Mr. Sawada and Kozuko. Basically, the timing for any ticket buying was totally dependent on the Consulate's granting of the Fiance' Visa. It was reiterated that Mr. Sawada was his Mom's point of contact for all the details concerning Koz once the MC GOVERN got underway... which would happen in now; two days! This was to be Joey's last phone call home but he did give the telegram and APL Company addresses of the Liberty to his Mom and to Sawada San for their use in contacting him in case of late-breaking, but important, news.

Kozuko was unsmiling but fully understanding as to why Joey needed to leave their apartment. She knew he had to return to the ship to help complete underway preparations for the ship's return trip across the Pacific. She accepted the money Joey left with her, with the comment that it would be deposited in the local bank until needed for her trip, East. In reviewing the bidding up to that point, Joey felt he had covered all possibilities on getting Koz to the States, and he liked that feeling.

The last two days the ship spent in Onomichi were trying from the standpoint of inventorying all goods loaded aboard against the listing of "Ordered Items". The probability of something important being overlooked (missing) was very high. Sure enough, Pearl Harbor Charts, because of their security classification, were not included in the "needed navigational data" package. The engineering people on board, while missing a few repair parts, had little interest in this problem, but, since the Skipper made a "big thing" over it… "concern", per se, infected the entire crew. The Chief Engineer did not want to go through what the Mates were going through with the Captain, so he loudly proclaimed over the sound-powered phone to the bridge; "… the Engineering Department is fully ready to get underway!" In thinking it through, with only a few reservations, Joey agreed with the Chief's proclamation.

It should also be known that this proclamation was delivered a bit early. The major factor standing in the way of being ready for "an underway" included: *Prior to undocking the dock had to be flooded.* This flooding was of concern because of the huge number of bottom plates and double bottom tanks that were repaired (after being damaged in the grounding) plus the meticulous attention given (repairs made) to) the ship's strakes, keel and longitudinal strips of steel-beaming that line the hull from forward, aft. That said; the below decks integrity had to be insured by a "leak-check" to be made by the ship's crew. This "check" was both important and extensive! Repeating; all this checking and repair- follow-up had to have been accomplished prior to the Chief's proud announcement.

The second consideration on "being ready to get underway" had to include *the complete loading of engineering and deck consumables …and repair parts.* In addition to the consumables used in overhauling the main engine, engine subsystems and auxiliary machinery repairs accomplished while in dock also used an inordinate amount of separately stocked, consumable material and designated spare parts. All replacements had to have been ordered and then properly stowed upon receipt. They were!

Also, there *had to be witnessed, operational tests that were completed on the installed, ship's steering (rudder) system.* That system had to be fully operational and depended upon the ship's boilers being on the line providing the steam used in its operation. It tested easily and the test was determined to be "satisfactory"!

Finally, *there had to have been light-off tests made to the boilers.* The temporary and portable tanks stowed topside were "the Fuel Tanks On Service". These provided the top-off oil to the (undamaged during the grounding) Fuel Oil-Settling Tanks in the boiler room, that actually fed the boilers. This entire subsystem had to be in operation and the boilers "making steam" prior to the flooding of the dock. It was!

Also under the "Fuel Oil" heading, prior to the dock flooding, *the fuel to be used for propulsion of the ship had to be standing by and awaiting the undocking, … and the ship being in an anchorage prior to its leaving Japan for the States.* Two harbor fuel barges were tied to a tug and standing by to seaward of the dock entrance!

The Chief Engineer was accurate; the MC GOVERN was, from an engineering standpoint, ready to get underway. While it was relatively late in the day, the decision was to undock and proceed to a nearby anchorage to finish the load-out. Using a loudspeaker system announcement to that effect, all hands were alerted to the dock being reflooded. The Docking and Harbor Pilots were both on the bridge and a medium-sized Japanese tug boat was standing by at the dock entrance to assist as needed in the undocking and anchoring.

Extreme care was exercised in flooding the graving dock. No one wished to have the Liberty do anything but gently and vertically rise off "the blocks" she rested upon these past few weeks. "Gently" became the operative word. It was almost "evening star time" when the dock flooding was completed and it was fully "night time" and dark when the ship proceeded to anchorage. The load-out was delayed until daylight the following day.

Upon hearing of the planning to anchor, and then shift to the "load-out mode" in the morning, the drydock company, Mitsubishi Iron Works, made a small "personnel carrier" boat available to the ship for the night. That ship-planning was not lost to Joey either. He immediately asked for permission to go ashore following the anchoring, with the proviso that he'd be back aboard for his mid-watch. All three in the decision making order; the Second Assistant Engineer, the Chief and the Captain all OK'd his liberty.

Joey left the ship and pointed himself directly to the apartment he ensconced Koz in. Upon his arrival, Sawada San waved to him in greeting and Koz was found hosting Slim's geisha for dinner. Upon seeing him in the doorway, Koz forgot all about everything else and literally jumped into Joey's arms. Joey was again surprised at how small

Koz was. He hugged her in a "protective manner" and kissed her several times before releasing her.

Slim's geisha, Kozuko's friend and partner from the Cherry Blossom House, became quite nervous upon Joey's arrival and with a meaningful "Sayonara!" she departed the apartment. Koz just waived " a farewell" at her and then gave Joey her entire attention. Kozuko, upon being released from the hug, let Joey know that now with her guest gone, he'd be able to have dinner right there in the apartment. A fair sized, gutted and scaled snapper-type fish was wrapped in a copy of the local newspaper, the Onomichi Shinbun, …and being roasted in the hibachi. Joey thought it interesting that after having been marinated in soy sauce, the fish had a wonderful "Japanese food" aroma. Joey hadn't really thought about it but he was hungry!

Over dinner they discussed Joey's ability to have made it ashore from the anchored ship, and then recapped their plans for Kozuko's upcoming trip to the States, and also the roll being played by "their Lawyer" and landlord, Sawada San. Koz had had complete faith and trust in the man for several years and these feelings were now reinforced by the man's roll and actions at their wedding. Koz also thanked Joey for formalizing her introduction to Joey's Mom… and how happy it made her, Kozuko, to be accepted into Joey's family. Joey made a mental note to insure he passed along Koz's feelings to his Mom, and to thank her for imparting this feeling to Koz. All were extremely important actions to Joey at this point. He knew that once he left Onomichi his relationship with Koz was totally out of his control and he wanted that relationship to continue as it currently existed. He loved this girl and wanted to share his life with her. To her credit, Koz knew this and abetted Joey's feeling!

It was surprising to Joey that he and Koz talked so much and for so long that they did not have time for (departing) love making. For the final time, Joey went over their financial arrangements just prior to his having to return to the waterfront and the personnel carrier boat awaiting him.

His final hug and kiss with her had him teary. He tried fighting that feeling as being "…less than a manly reaction". Before he walked through the apartment door he succumbed and cried openly. His departure was not a happy one.

The following morning at 7 AM the ship stationed the Anchor Detail, weighed anchor and set sail for the open Pacific Ocean. At the ship's top speed of 11 knots, the trip to Hawaii promised to be a long one. It was a clear day so Joey watched the scenery as the ship cleared the final, Easterly point of land at Onomichi. The residential housing on the hill and that portion of the hill set aside for the Cherry Blossom Festival both looked asleep in the early morning haze. Finally, when his apartment was obscured by the graving dock entrance, Joey lost interest in sightseeing. And when the Town shrunk into the horizon-dominated, relatively flat landscape of Hiroshima Prefecture, Joey gave in to his hunger and made it into the Mess Deck for breakfast.

Joey took his regular place at the table, next to Slim, and ordered his standard meal from Otis, mumbling under his breath that; "...it'd be great if somebody aboard this bucket knew how to bake bagels." His next thoughts went to the 76 beat per minute reciprocating main engine vibrating under his feet. "Feel that thing banging away down there? Gonna be a long trip!" Joey smilingly mused aloud. Slim smiled in return.

The End

ABOUT THE AUTHOR

Howard Venezia is a retired Captain, US Navy, and Master (unlimited Tonnage and Waters) of the US Merchant Marine. As described in this book, Liberty Ship Trip, he personally made the voyage described and is a veteran of the Korean War. He writes drawing from his general experience as a merchant seaman and from recalling the actual shipboard environment experienced on board a Liberty ship in a voyage from Beaumont, Texas to Pusan, Korea during the Korean War. His shipboard background is complete and includes "sailing" the world's oceans in both shipboard Deck and Engine billets over a 48 year seagoing career. He knows whereof he speaks of these venues and in descriptions of the seamen making these trips. He was there.